12 DATES OF CHRISTMAS

Christmas Falls: Season 2

BRIGHAM VAUGHN

Two Peninsulas Press

Editing by Rebecca Fairfax

Formatting by Brigham Vaughn

Cover design ©Morningstar Ashley Designs

Reindeer Illustration ©Nadia Telegina

Printed in the United States of America

First Printing 2024

AUTHOR'S NOTE

I was so excited to delve into the world of Christmas Falls once again!

Huge thanks to DJ Jamison for organizing it and I had a wonderful time working on the series with DJ, Beth, Lee, Rye, Amy, J.A., Lisa, Kelly, Rhys, and Hayden.

Thank you to Sandy Bennett for your help plotting the story and generally keeping me sane.

Thank you to Allison Hickman and Lynnette Brisia for your beta feedback as always.

Thank you to Rebecca Fairfax for your edits, and thank you to Julie Fouts Hansen, Melissa Womochil, and Rye Cox for your proofreading.

I appreciate all of your hard work!

Thank you to Lauren Kohout for naming Gumdrop! It was the perfect name for a reindeer.

AUTHOR'S NOTE

As always, a big thank you to all of you readers who make this possible. Without you, I wouldn't be living my dream of being a full-time author.

Happy Reading!

TABLE OF CONTENTS

BOOK BLURB vii

CHAPTER ONE 1
CHAPTER TWO 9
CHAPTER THREE 24
CHAPTER FOUR 40
CHAPTER FIVE 51
CHAPTER SIX 63
CHAPTER SEVEN 86
CHAPTER EIGHT 100
CHAPTER NINE 116
CHAPTER TEN 123
CHAPTER ELEVEN 141
CHAPTER TWELVE 150
CHAPTER THIRTEEN 171
CHAPTER FOURTEEN 181
CHAPTER FIFTEEN 194
CHAPTER SIXTEEN 202
CHAPTER SEVENTEEN 217
CHAPTER EIGHTEEN 234
CHAPTER NINETEEN 247
EPILOGUE 259

MORE CHRISTMAS FALLS 265
BRIGHAM'S BOOKS 267
ABOUT THE AUTHOR 277

BOOK BLURB

Leo Fenner needs a Christmas miracle …

Charmed by the small town, and weary of the big city dating scene, Leo moved to Christmas Falls in hopes of finding love like his college friend, Hayden.

Nick Morgan had the love of his life and lost her, but is determined to help others find their happily ever after with his matchmaking service.

His website needs work though, and Leo is just the man for the job.

The web developer signs up for Nick's matchmaking service to get a feel for what the process is like, all while secretly hoping it'll bring him the love of his dreams.

But as Nick and Leo work together, the sparks between them are impossible to ignore.

Too bad there's a few little problems.

For one, Nick's never fallen for a man before. And, oh yeah—those dates he's planning for Leo? They're supposed to be with other guys …

Christmas Falls: Season 2 revisits a small town that thrives on enough holiday charm to rival any Hallmark movie. It's a multi-author M/M romance series.

Content Warning: Discussion of a past death of a spouse and grief.

1. Sugar Plum Park
2. Dancing Sugar Plums
3. Santa's Workshop
4. Nutcrackers
5. Ginger's Breads
6. Tidings & Joy
7. Santa's Helpers Animal Shelter
8. Frosty's
9. Gingerbread Cottage
10. Jolly Java
11. Holiday Hope Foundation
12. Jingle Bites
13. Town Hall
14. The White Elephant
15. The Snowflake Shack
16. Mistletoe Movies
17. Christmas Falls Festivals Inc
18. Festival Museum
19. Rudolph's
20. Season's Readings

CHAPTER ONE

"I hate you a little bit." Leo Fenner sighed and set a box on the coffee table.

Hayden Bradley smirked. "Nice thing to say to your best friend who's helping you move into your new place."

Leo grinned. "Okay, fine. I don't *hate* you. But I am jealous. How did you manage to snag the *perfect* guy?"

"Slipped and fell on my ass in front of his bakery," Hayden said with a laugh. "And then was rude to him."

"Yeah, I dunno that I can recreate that one." Laughing too, Leo dropped onto the couch in his new apartment.

The one right above that very same bakery, Ginger's Breads.

Hayden had met his boyfriend, Joel MacArthur, last winter in a way that seemed like something out of a cute little holiday rom-com movie.

Hayden had moved from Chicago to the small town of Christmas Falls, Illinois to temporarily live with his mom and stepdad while he desperately tried to find a job as a web designer. His goal was to get the hell out of town as fast as possible. Instead, he'd been swept off his feet by the bakery owner, found a gig working as a website designer for the local college, and been hired to revamp the town's festival website.

Which was where Leo had come in.

At the time, he'd been living in Chicago and working for a big company as a web developer. When people got the two jobs confused—and they always did—Leo had always liked to joke that Hayden made websites pretty, but he made them *work.*

Which wasn't *entirely* true but it made Hayden get that grumpy look on his face that always made Leo laugh.

Hayden had texted him in a panic late last winter and said he needed help with a misbehaving section of the website, Leo had pitched in. What he'd expected to be a one-time-thing had turned into a semi-regular freelance gig.

While Leo could have done it all remotely, he'd used it as an excuse to visit his friend. Every time he was here, he fell a little more in love with the quirky little town that celebrated Christmas 24/7, 365 days a year.

"Hey, you okay?" Hayden asked with a frown. "You seem a little quiet. I thought you'd be more excited about moving here."

"I am," Leo protested. "Just … I don't know. It suddenly feels a little crazy to realize I totally uprooted my life in Chicago to move to some Christmas-themed small town on the off chance of finding love."

He laughed after he said that aloud because it *was* ridiculous sounding. But here he was.

"I get that," Hayden said, perching on the arm of the sofa. "But you have to admit, there's something about this place that seems to bring people together."

"There is," Leo agreed.

Because in the past ten months he'd spent driving from Chicago to Christmas Falls to hang out with Hayden and do the work on the Christmas Festival's website together, he heard the stories about how people met. He saw all of the adorable couples strolling down Candy Cane Lane. He watched several first dates and even a *proposal* happen before his very eyes!

And Leo wanted that. He wanted it *so bad* but he was getting nowhere in Chicago. Not with the dating apps. Not going to queer spaces. Not at cheesy speed-dating events.

Chicago's thriving neighborhood of Boystown should have been the easiest place in the world to find the guy of his dreams. But nope. Leo had been ghosted and lied to and even *scammed*. Yeah, that had been his breaking point.

That was the moment he'd said fuck it and started aggressively planning to move to Christmas Falls.

Leo glanced over at Hayden, who was staring with a worried frown. "I'll be okay," he said lightly. "It'll all work out eventually."

Because he *had* to believe that or he'd throw himself into a snowbank and refuse to ever come out.

"Okay." Leo slapped his thighs, then rose to his feet. "Let's get the rest of this stuff moved in, then you can take me out to lunch at Frosty's."

Hayden snorted. "Uhh, pretty sure you're supposed to take *me* out since I was the one who helped you move."

Leo shrugged, following him to the door. "Potato-potahto," he said breezily.

As they walked down the steps, they ran into Joel.

Leo stifled an appreciative sigh. The man was a hunky ginger-haired bear of a baker with kind eyes and a sweet smile. Lucky Hayden.

"It's slowed down a little at the bakery so I can help you guys unload, if you want," Joel said, flashing that same sweet smile at them both before he bent to give Hayden a quick kiss, wrapping an arm around his waist.

Hayden shot him an adoring look and Leo had to look away. They were utterly, disgustingly in love.

Leo was *so* fucking envious.

"Thanks, Joel. Help would be amazing," Leo said gratefully. He'd sold most of his furniture since the apartment over the bakery came with the pieces he needed, but he still had plenty of crap to haul upstairs.

Thankfully, with three people, the work was a whole lot lighter than it had been when Leo packed the car in Chicago by himself. Although, if Leo caught Hayden ogling Joel's ass one more time, he was going to barf.

Or maybe that was the envy talking again. Because goddamn did Joel have a nice ass.

Joel should use that for the bakery's tagline: home of the baker with the best buns.

Twenty minutes later, Leo's car was empty, his thighs ached from the trips up and down the stairs, and a plate of warm ginger-molasses cookies from the bakery sat on the coffee table.

"You didn't have to do that," Leo protested, but he was already eagerly reaching for one of Joel's incredible treats. "You gave me your apartment."

Joel grinned. "I wouldn't call having a rental agreement *giving* it to you, but of course I had to get you a housewarming gift! You're officially a resident of Christmas Falls!"

Leo bit into the cookie and tried not to moan. No wonder Hayden had fallen in love with the baker. He wasn't just hot. These cookies were *legit.* Chewy and sweet, with a bite of ginger that made his tongue tingle.

As if Hayden could tell what Leo was thinking, he slid an arm around Joel's waist and eyed Leo. "Don't go getting any ideas though. This guy is all mine."

Leo laughed and nearly choked on his cookie. "I know *that,*" he mumbled around his food.

After he finished the last delicious bite, he glanced between Hayden and Joel. "Seriously, I'm happy for you guys. I love that you got a house together."

Hayden beamed, which said everything because he had been a horrible grump last year. Though, who could blame him? He'd been through a lot. "Yeah, I'm excited we found a place."

Joel had lived over the bakery for about a decade and Hayden had moved in with him last winter. A few months ago, they'd found a cute little house on the edge of downtown and had slowly been moving in there.

That was when Leo had, mostly jokingly, said something about moving to Christmas Falls and taking over the apartment. Joel had brightened, looking excited. He'd quoted a price so low Leo nearly fell over.

Once the idea had been planted in Leo's head, it refused to budge. He'd paid three times more in Chicago and his job could be done remotely except for the occasional trip into the office every few months.

Christmas Falls seemed like a fairytale compared to Chicago so why not?

But he hadn't been serious about it until a few weeks later when the guy he'd gone on a few dates with had given him a sob story about being kicked out of the house he was renting with friends.

There had been tears as he'd told about his former housemates throwing slurs at him as they tossed his belongings on the lawn. The guy had seemed so scared and traumatized that Leo knew he had to help.

While Leo wasn't comfortable letting a virtual stranger move in with him, he'd given him enough money to rent a clean—if not fancy—hotel room for a week until he got housing straightened out.

Only a few days later, when the guy went silent and Leo mentioned it to a friend over brunch, the friend rolled his eyes. "Yeah, you haven't heard about that old scam going around the area?" he said, pity dripping from his voice and written all over his face. "I can't *believe* you fell for it. You're so naïve."

Leo had looked online and found proof it had happened to dozens of guys in the area.

So yeah, that was the last fucking straw. That same night, he'd video chatted with Hayden and Joel about the logistics for moving into their old place while he packed his belongings.

Fuck the Chicago dating scene.

Leo deserved real love. Not people who would use real, awful situations *actually* happening to queer people as some ploy to scam money out of them.

"Leo? You're coming to Thanksgiving dinner next week, right?" Joel asked now. "We're excited to host it for the first time."

"Yep. I'll be there!" Leo promised. "Want me to bring a side dish?"

"Please," Joel answered with a smile. "We've got the turkey, stuffing, and obviously the pies are all taken care of."

They all laughed.

The man could cook *and* bake. Seriously, Hayden had all the luck.

"One green bean casserole coming up!" Leo promised brightly, because he refused to be resentful of his friend's happiness.

"Great," Hayden said. "This'll be fun!"

"It will. But I should head downstairs again. Sorry I can't help you get settled in more, Leo." Joel looked apologetic. "We're ramping up to the holidays and …"

"Yeah, no worries, I get it," Leo assured him. "Trust me. This won't take too long to unpack. You were both a huge help already."

Hayden glanced at his phone. "I think we'll work for about an hour on getting Leo organized, then head to lunch."

"Okay," Joel said, dropping a kiss on Hayden's lips. "See you at home in a few hours?"

"Yep, I'll see you then."

"Love you!"

"Love you too."

But before Joel could go, Hayden reached out and grabbed his shirt. He kissed him a little more thoroughly, winding his arms around Joel's neck.

A pang of envy appeared again.

Hayden *glowed* whenever he was around Joel or even talked about him. And Joel glowed right back.

It was everything Leo had ever wanted and—damn it—this was his year to find it!

He was ready for his own Christmas miracle.

CHAPTER TWO

Nicholas Morgan straightened the pens inside the green glass cup on his desk, oddly nervous about the upcoming meeting.

He'd spent the past month working virtually with Leo Fenner to update his website but they hadn't actually spoken face-to-face yet. Leo had moved to town a few days ago and had emailed Nick asking if they could have their upcoming meeting in person.

Nick had said yes because Leo had been a lifesaver already.

Nick had started the matchmaking business last year, mostly operating on word of mouth and a few poorly cobbled together Google forms. He had tried to build a website himself, signing up for one advertised as "easy to put together in minutes!" but that was a lie. At least for him. He had no idea what he was doing and had quickly gotten in over his head.

It didn't do half of the stuff he wanted, and what he'd managed to do looked like garbage.

Nick had reached out to Hayden Bradley for help but he'd taken one look at what Nick wanted, then frowned and shook his head.

"I think you need a web developer. I can make your site look pretty but some of the functionality you want is … well, I'll be honest. It's beyond my skills. I know *some* coding but you want to integrate the in-depth questionnaire and scheduling into your site—you need someone who can build it from scratch and personalize it to your needs. I have a friend I went to college with who does some freelance work though, if you're interested. He does top-notch, professional work and he's not crazy expensive."

Hayden had given Leo's email address to Nick but Nick had been a little embarrassed to email Leo about what a mess he'd made.

He'd put it off for weeks, but once he finally did it and got a response back, he'd regretted dragging his feet. Leo had been kind and funny in their email interactions, and had immediately put Nick at ease.

After Nick hired Leo, he'd filled out spreadsheets and forms with all kinds of information about his business and what he was looking for.

He loved what Leo had created so far.

But the *About Me* section was where Nick kept getting stuck. How could he put into words why he'd felt the need to do this?

Why he wanted to help other people find love.

Nick had tried to put a positive spin on the situation, but frankly, it *was* a little depressing to remind potential clients the love of his life was gone. He'd scare people away, reminding them that even if they were lucky enough to find their soulmate, it didn't mean they'd grow old together.

With a sigh, Nick sat back and looked around the cozy office Nicole had used to write her books.

They'd put the addition on the house a few years before her death. She'd been a prolific romance author and once her books had taken off, they'd agreed she desperately needed a dedicated office space instead of her desk being crammed into the narrow spare bedroom.

The addition had turned out beautifully with a wide desk, a cozy reading chair, and walls of bookshelves Nick had built for her.

Sorting through and donating Nicole's clothing and tossing her toiletries with the help of her brother, Ford Donnely, had been gut-wrenching, but dismantling *this* space filled to the brim with reminders of her and her work had felt impossible. The room had sat nearly untouched for more than a year after her death, until Nick's older sister had finally held his hand through the process.

But as Nick had sorted through letters from Nicole's fans and read how her stories had encouraged them to be brave and find love, an idea had begun to grow. An idea to start a matchmaking service.

A way to help other people find the love Nick and Nicole had shared.

It had felt cathartic to build something and his sister, Heather, had pushed him to keep going whenever he got doubtful.

And now, bittersweet as it was, the office space was all his.

He'd slowly redecorated it, keeping the cream-colored walls and the sturdy oak desk, but swapping out the light, gauzy curtains for heavier drapes.

Instead of Nicole's framed book cover art, there were photos he'd taken of Lake Michigan and other places they'd visited on vacation together.

He'd switched out the smaller green chair she'd curled up in to read for a bigger brown leather chair and ottoman better suited to his height. One shelf was still dedicated to every book Nicole had ever written but it was right next to the thrillers and mysteries Nick devoured.

It had felt right to merge the old with the new, to remember the past without clinging to every last scrap of it.

The exterior door that led to the backyard had allowed Nicole to wander outside when she was feeling stuck on a story. It was now the perfect entrance where Nick could welcome his clients, rather than making them traipse through his house.

Which reminded him Leo would be arriving any minute. A stab of guilt went through Nick. He still hadn't finished the bio for the website.

He'd written and re-written it dozens of times, driving himself crazy in the process, but he could never seem to find the right words.

He smiled, fond sadness sweeping over him. Nicole would have had the perfect words. She'd have turned his pathetic attempts into something beautiful and heartfelt.

But while Nick was talented at woodworking and photography—the latter of which had turned out to be surprisingly handy when helping clients build their matchmaking profiles

—and skilled at knowing which couples would likely hit it off, writing was *not* his forte.

A quick rap of knuckles on the door made Nick straighten. He cleared his throat and stood. Hopefully Leo wouldn't be too upset that he hadn't finished what he'd promised to do.

Nick swung open the door to find a young man on the other side dressed in nice trousers, a sweater, and an unzipped parka.

He had the most striking face Nick had ever seen.

Nick stared at him for a moment before he blinked. "Uh, hey. You must be Leo. Come in."

He held the door for Leo, who walked up a few steps and beamed as he held out a hand. "Great to finally meet you, Nick."

Huh. Leo didn't look exactly like Nick had expected. For some reason, Nick had pictured him as short and mousy with glasses. Maybe some patchy facial hair and an awkward, shy demeanor. Of course, Nick was probably buying into the stereotypes about what computer geeks looked like. Guiltily, he realized he shouldn't assume anything.

Hell, look at Jett Davis. He was one of Nick's clients who lived in town, worked as a coder, and was, by pretty much any standard, very good-looking.

Leo was too. He was tall—meeting Nick's gaze at the same level—and Nick was 6'2". He was slender but strong looking. His face was clean-shaven, his smile was dazzling and his grip was warm and firm as they shook.

"Let me get your coat," Nick said, swallowing hard as he shook Leo's hand.

Leo set a laptop bag on the nearby chair, then shrugged out of the parka. Nick took it and hung it on the antique hooks he'd installed beside the door recently.

Nick had guessed Leo would be about Hayden's age since they'd gone to school together but it hit him suddenly that Leo was only in his mid-twenties. It made Nick feel ancient.

He'd fallen in love, gotten married, and been widowed already.

Granted, he was only thirty-eight now, but he felt a hell of a lot older than the fresh-faced web developer in front of him. But grief would do that to a person.

"How's moving in going?" Nick asked.

"Oh, great! I don't own that much and it's a small apartment so it's been easy. Plus, they left me some furniture. I think all I need to buy is a desk."

"If you're into antiques or thrift stores, I could recommend a few in the area," Nick offered. "Merry Memories is outside of town and it's my favorite."

Leo's face lit up. "Oh, that would be great! I'm tired of cheap Ikea shit."

That smile transformed his look. His face was a little angular, with a long straight nose, strong chin and full mouth. He suddenly reminded Nick of a slightly younger version of the model Nicole had used as inspiration for the main character in one of her stories, *A Model Husband*.

Nicole had laughed when Nick had walked past her computer and stopped dead in his tracks at the sight of the guy on her screen. "Damn. Who's that?" he'd asked.

"Inspo for Damien in the new book."

"Well, I can see why Kenzie falls for him."

She'd grinned and swatted at him, then told him to get out of her office and stop distracting her.

He felt a small, familiar pang of missing Nicole before he refocused on Leo. His light brown hair was a tousled mess as he took off his hat and stuffed it into the sleeve of his hanging parka, still smiling.

"Wow, great office," he said, glancing around, blue eyes dancing. He smoothed down his hair. "I *love* the vibes."

"Yeah?" Nick said, a little amused by the enthusiasm. Leo had seemed friendly and warm over email, but he hadn't expected the bright, cheery tones and bubbly mood.

"It feels nice." Leo shrugged. "Dunno, can't explain it."

"Well, thank you," Nick managed. "I, uh, it's a special space for me."

They stared at each other for a moment until Nick cleared his throat. "How do we want to do this?"

'This' being their meeting about the final details of the website.

Leo shrugged. "I was thinking I'd get out my laptop, you can take a look at the changes I made since the latest feedback you sent, then we can go from there?"

"Sounds great," Nick agreed. "Feel free to set up at my desk."

It was a giant slab of oak with four straight narrow legs and two shallow drawers at the top so there was plenty of room for two computers and chairs.

Leo looked it over. "Great desk too."

Nick smiled. "Thanks. It was made nearly a hundred years ago. It belonged to the local library and they sold it when they did some remodeling. My wife and I got it at the antique place I mentioned. Merry Memories."

"Very cool." Leo unpacked his laptop and set it on one end of the desk. "Will this work? I think it's the only spot where my cord will reach the outlet. Sorry, I need a new battery. It dies after about twenty minutes of being unplugged."

"Sure. We can move the other chair around." Nick lugged the chair to the other side of the desk, then slipped into his own, the chairs pressed right up against one another.

Leo fussed with a few things before he got situated, his forearm brushing Nick's as he typed in his login. "Okay, so this should be all queued up for you."

Nick listened intently as Leo walked him through the website, from the landing page to the how matchmaking works section, and finally to the in-depth questionnaires people filled out with their preferences.

"And here's the booking section where people can set up appointments for their in-person interviews with you. I think it makes sense for you to stick to local matchmaking for now but if you do eventually decide you want to expand and do this on a larger scale, we can change the wording and add an option for video chats."

"Perfect," Nick said, smiling. "That's so much better than what I had."

"You mean a badly done Google form and you sending eighteen emails back and forth with your client trying to find a time you both have free?" Leo teased. "No! You don't say."

Nick made a face but chuckled, nodding. "Yeah. Yeah. Well, there's a reason I hired you!"

Leo grinned. It was a little crooked and made a dimple in his right cheek pop out. Nick glanced away, clearing his throat.

"Good thing you did! I'm amazed you had any clients at all with what you were working with before."

Nick chuckled. "Honestly, it helps that it's a small town," he admitted. "I've been relying on word of mouth."

"Hey, I'm not knocking it. And the customer testimonials you included are great," Leo said. "Clearly you know what you're doing. But this new site will give your clients a central place to go to get all of the information they need and you'll have to do *way* less work going back and forth with them via email. And, again, if and when you're ready, the framework will be in place for you to expand to a larger market."

"Fantastic." Nick hesitated. "And you'll maintain the website? For a fee, of course. I'm happy to pay whatever your usual rate is."

"Of course," Leo said with a wink, then grew serious. "But, yeah, we can definitely do that. And I can make tweaks whenever you need—just try to give me a heads-up so I can work you into my schedule. If you need something added, if you want to change stuff seasonally—"

"What do you mean by that?" Nick asked, frowning.

Leo clicked over to the home page. "You see right here?" He gestured to the top of the page.

Nick leaned in to get a better look, his elbow bumping Leo's.

"We could swap the current banner for something seasonal. Like … lots of people get lonely around the holidays. We could do a wintery image with a tagline about finding someone to snuggle up with around the fire. Then swap the image and talk about taking vacations together in the summer … that sort of thing."

"I do like the idea," Nick admitted.

"Okay." Leo typed something into his phone. "Done."

"Just like that?" Nick asked, amused.

Leo nodded. "Just like that. It'll take me like half an hour tops, when I get home."

"That's great. I'm honestly impressed with your work," Nick admitted. He would have been leery of hiring someone a few years out of college but Hayden's work had been stellar and he'd trusted his recommendation of Leo.

The kid knew what he was doing.

"Thanks!" Leo beamed. "This was a fun project to work on. My day job is sooo boring. Hayden maybe has a great point about how nice it is working with smaller clients instead of giant corporations."

"Yeah?" Nick asked.

Leo shrugged. "I mean, whatever. My day job is fine. It pays the bills and I can work remotely so I can't complain too much. But setting up a page to sell more yoga pants to people who already own twenty pairs isn't as rewarding as helping people find the love of their life, you know?"

Nick smiled. "Sure. That makes sense to me. I quit my job as a loan officer to do this." He gestured at the site.

"Oh yeah?"

"Yep. It was hard, crushing people's dreams when I had to turn them down."

Leo winced. "That does sound sucky. You must have said yes sometimes too though, right?"

"Oh definitely," Nick agreed, twisting a little in his chair so he could see Leo's face better. "I did. And I loved that. Hell, one of the last loans I offered was for Hayden and Joel's new place, which was a great feeling. It … it got tiring when there were too many 'No's', however."

"I get that."

They both fell silent for a moment.

"We're close to being done," Leo said as he sat back. "I still need a few things from you though."

"I know." Nick reached up, rubbing the back of his neck. Damn it, they'd arrived at the part of the meeting he'd been dreading. "I'm dragging my heels on the bio."

"If you're not sure what to write, I could show you some examples of other matchmaking sites. Maybe that would help?" Leo offered earnestly.

But Nick shook his head. "No, that's not it. I mean, I tried that already. The problem isn't me having no idea about what I should say. It's just … it's difficult for me."

"Okay," Leo said slowly. "I'm not quite sure I understand but …"

Nick sighed. "The truth is, I lost my wife, Nicole, three-and-a-half years ago. It was very unexpected. She had a heart defect no one knew about and she was gone very quickly." He swallowed past the thickening in his throat. "She was the love of my life and I wanted to start this service because—because I hope other people can find love too."

"I think that's admirable," Leo said quietly. "That such a big loss has inspired you to do something kind for other people instead of letting it make you cynical."

Nick smiled faintly. "I still believe in love. I feel very lucky to have found it. Even if I only had it for fifteen years, I'll never regret it."

"The whole better to have loved and lost than never to have loved at all idea?" Leo asked with a gentle smile.

"Basically," Nick agreed. "I mean, it's definitely trite but at the heart of it all, that's how I feel." He glanced at the framed photo on his desk of their wedding day.

Leo's gaze followed his and he reached out but didn't touch the frame. "May I?"

"Yeah, of course."

Leo studied the photo for a few minutes. "She's lovely. And I know it's only a photo but she looks … really kind."

"She was." Nick smiled, then cleared his throat. "Anyway, you see why I'm dragging my heels on writing this. I worry my story is too depressing."

"No, not at all," Leo said, carefully returning the photo to its place on Nick's desk. "I think you should include it."

"Yeah?" Nick was doubtful.

"Definitely. Do you mind if I take a look at what you have so far?"

"No, not at all." Nick leaned forward and jiggled his mouse.

"I have it up here in a doc. I was trying to work on it before you got here."

"Oh, cool."

Nick opened his mouth to offer Leo his seat but he was already standing. He stepped behind Nick and leaned forward, bracing his arms on the back of Nick's chair.

He smelled nice.

It was subtle. Nick hadn't noticed it earlier. But it reminded him of a cool winter day.

The kind where the sun was bright—bouncing off the snow in bright little rainbows of light—and the air was fresh and crisp and alive. There was something woodsy to the scent too, like fresh-cut pine trees.

Then Leo exhaled, brushing Nick's ear and cheek in a warm gust. Nick shivered.

"Oh I love this," Leo murmured. "What a great line."

"Which one?" It came out sounding a little funny.

"'I believe love is one of life's greatest joys.' So good! Hmm, can we tweak the last part a little bit though?"

"Sure," Nick said with a shrug.

Leo reached out, leaning forward, his arms coming around Nick's shoulders.

He typed quickly, his fingers flying over the keyboard, but Nick couldn't focus on the screen in front of him to see what he was writing. He was suddenly aware of Leo's arms around him, warm and surprisingly strong.

God, when was the last time someone had touched him? Someone who wasn't his *family*, wasn't a longtime friend.

Nick suddenly felt warm, like the temperature had gone up a few degrees.

"How's that?" Leo drew back.

Nick cleared his throat again and leaned forward. He read it silently, then nodded. "Yeah, that's great. I like that."

"Awesome." Leo rested a hand on his shoulder. "What's next?"

"In this bio?"

"Yeah."

Nick scrolled down a little to the final paragraph.

"Okay, hmm. Looks good. I have one more tiny tweak," Leo murmured as he leaned in, his breath dancing over the side of Nick's jaw. "And *there*."

"Great. That's perfect."

"We should be good to go now, as long as you're happy with the tweaks I made to your bio," Leo said, shifting away and dropping into his chair again, gone so suddenly it was like he hadn't been there at all. "It's very good. You were close."

Nick blinked. "Yeah?"

"Yeah. I mean, once you're satisfied with the bio, you can drop the file in the shared drive. I'll add it to the page, then test the site. Make sure all of the forms are working properly. I'll set up a dummy account and fill everything out like I'm a new client. I just won't submit the payment." Leo laughed softly. "Though God knows, I probably *should* set up an account. I am so bad at finding dates for myself it's ridiculous." He shook his head.

"You should sign up for real! I mean, why not?" When Leo looked surprised, Nick hastily tacked on. "I wouldn't charge you for it, of course. You've been so patient with me being indecisive and it's the least I can do."

"Oh, no." Leo looked startled. "I'm happy to pay my own way."

"No, please. I insist," Nick said. "Besides, you're new to town. If you're serious about wanting to use my matchmaking service, this would be a *great* way for you to meet people."

Leo hesitated. "True. And, I mean, I really *do* want to find someone, but you don't have to—"

Nick shrugged. "I know I don't. But I *want* to. Please say yes."

Smiling, Leo shrugged. "Well, why not? That's why I'm here in Christmas Falls, after all."

"Yeah?" Nick asked.

"Yeah." Leo suddenly looked a little shy. "I moved here to find the love of my life."

CHAPTER THREE

"Do not lust after the straight widower," Leo muttered to himself as he walked down the sidewalk in front of Nick's house, heading back to his new apartment on foot. He could have driven but it was only about a ten-minute walk and Leo was used to going everywhere on foot in Chicago.

Leo sighed.

If only Nicholas Morgan wasn't the single most gorgeous man Leo had ever seen. Tall, dark, and handsome didn't even begin to cover it.

"And, you know, *straight*," he reminded himself under his breath. Gah!

The poor man was grieving his wife's death for fuck's sake! Leo had been the one making it weird by putting his arms around him.

He hadn't done it *intentionally*. He'd just had an idea of how to tweak Nick's bio and hadn't wanted to lose his train of thought.

Except, he nearly had.

He'd suddenly realized he had a handsome man in his arms and, well, he'd like to get *unprofessional* with him.

Nick had been super nice and hadn't acted weirded out or anything. But *still*! Just because Leo and Nick had more relaxed interactions than Leo typically did with the clients he worked with at the firm in Chicago didn't mean he should go putting his hands on Nick.

Leo had meant every word he'd said though.

He admired Nick wanting to help others find love, even though he'd lost it. Not only was he good-looking, he was a nice guy.

Bah. Too bad he was straight.

For a minute there, Leo had kinda *wondered* but he'd been there way too many times before. He'd crushed on the unavailable guys. The guys who were already in relationships. Guys who *seemed* flirty but definitely weren't interested in dating him. And it always ended in disaster.

It was so hard when Leo was a hopeless romantic. Every time he got his hopes up, thinking this time it would be different … but no. It never was.

Which was all the more reason to take Nick up on his offer of matchmaking.

He just had to ignore the disappointment he wasn't going to get matched with *Nick*.

When Leo reached the bakery, he debated if he should go around to the back and let himself in the private entrance, or go in through the front door and snag a pastry before he went upstairs.

He should peek his head in and see how busy it was inside. He could always work in the bakery. There he'd have a real table instead of trying to work from the couch or the teeny-tiny table Joel had used for his meals before he met Hayden.

It was a perfectly good dining table for one person but a lousy desk when Leo needed to spread out.

The bakery was quiet at the moment, with a few people in line and one person at the small cluster of tables near the front, soft music playing in the background.

There wasn't a lot of seating, but Joel offered free coffee, tea, hot chocolate, and Wi-fi to anyone who wanted it. People didn't even have to buy anything!

Leo shook his head. *I'd never see that shit in Chicago.*

He eyed the glass case as he waited his turn in line, salivating over the delicious-looking baked goods.

"What can I get for you today, Leo?" Cassie asked cheerfully when he reached the front of the line.

"Oh, a slice of the maple pear and ginger pie, please."

"One slice, coming right up! Do you want whipped cream with that?"

"Obviously!"

"Dumb question. I should know by now."

"Probably."

Whenever Leo had visited Christmas Falls, he'd stopped in the bakery to try something new. Apparently, Cassie knew he was a total fiend for whipped cream.

Oh well, there were worse reputations to have.

Thankfully, Leo's favorite spot was available, so after he paid, he carried his slice of pie and whipped cream to the small table and got comfortable. He fixed himself a cup of coffee and plugged in his laptop.

He was surprised to find he already had an email from Nick, thanking him for his help and letting him know the completed bio was in the shared drive.

Perfect.

Leo updated that, then alternated bites of pie and sips of coffee as he created a couple of seasonal banners for Nick. He didn't have the graphic design skills Hayden had, but he wasn't half-bad.

He sent the completed design to Nick to approve, then cleared away the plate and fork, refilled his coffee, and waved at Joel who was stocking shelves.

He waved back cheerfully.

When Leo took a seat again, he was surprised there was already a message from Nick in the chat they'd been using saying he loved them all. ***Any chance we could use all three?***

Like a rotating banner flipping between the images in a loop? Leo replied.

Yeah, exactly. I like having all three couples represented.

Leo smiled. Damn it, Nick was so fucking sweet.

When they'd started working together, Leo had kinda assumed that the matchmaking service would be geared primarily toward straight couples. He wasn't sure why, since the town had a thriving LGBTQ+ population, but even in

Chicago, straight was kinda the default for most of the companies out there.

But Nick's plan had been inclusive from the beginning. He welcomed any pairing of couples and there was an option for preferred pronouns in the initial client info section and so many other little touches showing he wanted to be LGBTQ+ friendly.

Leo had created three different banners with two same-sex couples and one straight one, figuring Nick would pick which he liked most, but he loved Nick's idea to rotate them. From the moment people landed on the home page, it would be a perfect indicator the service was queer-friendly.

I can definitely do that! Give me a few, he replied.

Thanks! You're amazing.

Gah, as if Leo's crush on him wasn't getting worse by the minute already …

Because, oh no, Nick wasn't simply handsome and kind and queer-friendly, he was funny and he treated every little thing Leo did on his website like it was amazing. Which was a hell of a nice change from his corporate job but making it very difficult for Leo to remember Nick was not an option.

Not to date, anyway.

The rotating banner was easy to add though, so Leo uploaded the photos to it, then sent Nick a link to show him what it looked like.

Love it! That's exactly what I had in mind, Nick sent back a few moments later.

Awesome! We're getting close to launch! Unless I

find any major bugs when I test it, we should be good to go.

After a few more brief exchanges, Leo decided he might as well get to work testing the site's functionality.

Putting himself into the mindset of being a potential client, Leo filled out all of his basic information, then moved on to the more in-depth client questionnaire he'd built for Nick.

The first question was simple.

I am interested in: women, men, other, no gender preference.

Leo selected men, hit next, then moved on to question two.

If I could use one positive attribute to describe myself, it would be: nerdy, caring, artistic, trustworthy, intellectual.

Leo debated. Caring, maybe?

Nerdy applied too but even though this question referred to it as a positive attribute, Leo wasn't so sure everyone saw it that way. It was cute Nick did though.

Leo was trustworthy, or he tried to be. And he'd done well in school but he wasn't sure if intellectual was how he identified.

So he clicked on caring and moved on to the next question.

My favorite thing to do when I get home from work is: check my social media, do something creative, spend time with family, watch TV or a movie, or relax, I'm exhausted.

He frowned. None of those, really? He checked his social media throughout the day and his job *was* creative.

He did like spending time with his family but they lived in Wisconsin on a dairy farm and didn't make it to Chicago often, so while Leo loved visiting when he was home for the holidays, he couldn't do it regularly.

He liked TV and movies alright and Hayden and Joel had gotten him watching hockey lately—*Go, Otters!*—but that was more of a late-night thing for him.

He wasn't usually exhausted after work either.

Honestly, he tended to *work* after work, since he had his day job and this freelance stuff he did on the side, but that wasn't an option.

And neither was what he usually did.

Leo wrote himself a reminder in his notes app to suggest Nick add an option for going out or an *other* option with a fill-in-the-blank section.

Because if Leo didn't have work to do, he liked being social.

He was looking forward to all of the festivals and events around this town, especially since the holidays would be kicking off soon. He couldn't wait for the tree lighting festival tomorrow.

Leo sighed, propping his chin on his hand as he imagined walking hand-in-hand with someone at the event, sipping warm peppermint cocoa. Sharing a kiss under the glow of Christmas lights.

Ooh, or closer to Christmas when there was some snow, they could cozy up together on one of the reindeer sleigh rides advertised on the Christmas Falls website Hayden designed …

Oh no! Leo straightened, guiltily realizing he'd totally been picturing Nick. *Whoops.*

Leo sighed and focused on his screen, choosing *spend time with family* as his answer because it was the closest to what he wanted before he moved on to the next question, determined to push Nick out of his mind.

He had to focus on finding someone *available*.

When Leo was done, he let out a satisfied little sigh and shut down his laptop.

Now he had to let Nick work his matchmaking magic …

"Hey, little brother! You look good!" Heather said, hugging Nick tightly as they met at Sugar Plum Park.

He hugged her back, then pulled away. "Thanks for sounding so surprised."

She laughed, her dark eyes twinkling as she adjusted her hand-knitted cap, which he'd knocked slightly askew. "No, I didn't mean to. Only … it's been a while since you've come to any of the holiday festivals. I was surprised when you called to see if we'd be here."

'We' being her wife, Edie, and their kids. Edie had stayed home tonight because one of the kids was feeling sick and the other one had decided they wanted to hang out with their friends.

He nodded, shrugging. "I know. It was hard the first few years though. I just … I wasn't ready yet."

There had been too many raw memories and he'd hated being the guy who brought down the mood of every holiday event.

Heather reached out and squeezed his hand. "I know."

"But it felt right this year," he said firmly.

"That's great! I'm glad."

"Thanks. How are you?"

"Oh, good," she said. "Christmas break can't come soon enough. The kids are already getting squirrely."

Nick chuckled. He wasn't sure if she meant her own or the ones she taught at the local middle school but he had no doubt both were wound up.

They spent a few minutes catching up before Nick spotted Leo standing alone near the table Ginger's Breads had set up.

"Oh, hey," Nick said. "I should go say hi to Leo."

Heather raised an eyebrow. "Who's that?"

"The guy who built my website."

She looked confused. "I thought he was in Chicago."

"He was when we started. He moved here like a week ago. He's friends with Hayden Bradley and he's renting the apartment over Ginger's Breads from him and Joel now."

"Oh, yeah. They bought a house together recently, right?"

"Yep. C'mon," Nick said with a tilt of his head. "I'll introduce you."

"Okay."

"Leo," Nick called out as they approached and he turned, a few cookie crumbs falling onto his parka from the half-eaten cookie in his mouth.

His eyes widened and he swallowed, coughing a little. "Nick!" he said in a strangled voice.

"Are you okay?" Nick asked, amused.

Leo coughed again, then held up a finger and took a sip of what smelled like mulled cider. "Yeah, sorry." He coughed again. "Just inhaled cookie crumbs down the wrong pipe. I'll be fine in a minute though."

"Glad we don't have to do the Heimlich," Nick joked. "Hi, by the way."

Leo grinned. "Hi."

Heather cleared her throat and Nick jerked, glancing guiltily over at his sister. *Shit.* He'd totally forgotten she was there.

"Leo, this is my sister, Heather Morgan. Heather, this is Leo Fenner. He built my website."

"Hi!" Leo said cheerfully. "Great to meet you, Heather."

She smiled. "You too. I understand you were living in Chicago and recently moved to Christmas Falls?"

"I did. Just in time for the Christmas Festival to kick off, apparently."

Heather laughed. "Well, there's no shortage of events around here if you enjoy them."

Leo beamed. "Oh, I do. I love it! It's so great. There are so many cute little events and the town is *adorable.*"

"We like it," Heather said. "Is the festival why you moved here? I mean, if you don't mind sharing. I don't want to be too nosy."

"No, you're good. Yeah, the festival is part of it. And I liked the whole vibe of the place."

Nick smiled. Leo was apparently big on vibes.

"And, you know, everyone in town seemed so friendly and welcoming. I'm kinda burned out on the big city scene, honestly."

"Yeah, I get that," Heather said. "I was glad when my wife and I moved back here."

"Okay," Leo leaned in. "Is it me or is this like the queerest little town ever? I mean, don't get me wrong, I love it! But I was surprised."

Heather nodded. "It's turned into a queer haven lately. I think all of the Christmas kitsch attracts a certain type."

"Yeah, I can see that." Leo grinned. "It's so great. Reminds me a little bit of Pendleton Bay. Have you ever been there?"

"Oh, the small town on the west side of Michigan? No, but I've heard great things."

"Super cute little town too," Leo said. "And very queer-friendly."

As Nick opened his mouth to mention he and Nicole had visited it a few years before her death, Hayden appeared.

"Oh, hey!" Leo said, grinning as he gave his friend a hug. "There you are."

Nick and Heather both greeted Hayden and they all made small talk for a few minutes. When Heather asked about the new house, Hayden glanced over at Joel, who was deep in conversation with a customer but glanced up, shooting Hayden a warm smile.

Nick smiled at their obvious affection.

It was nice to see the town baker settled down. He'd seemed happy running his bakery before Hayden came into his life but there was a certain impossible to ignore contented air around both of them now.

Rumor had it, Hayden had been incredibly grumpy before they met, although Nick hadn't gotten to know him until the two of them were already together.

The right relationship could definitely bring out the best in a person though. Which was *exactly* why Nick was determined to make this matchmaking business a success.

Heather tugged on Nick's sleeve. "Ooh, I think they're going to start soon. Want to get a good spot so you can take some photos?"

Nick smiled and gestured to the camera hanging around his neck. "How'd you guess?"

Leo and Hayden were deep in conversation now so Nick murmured a goodbye and got a distracted wave in answer.

"Seriously," Heather said as they walked away. "It's great to see you here. There's a lightness around you I haven't seen in a while."

"Well, I think getting the website up and running is helping too. Leo launched the page this morning and we already have our first signup!"

Two, technically, if Nick counted Leo's profile. He'd spent a while reading through what Leo was looking for and had written down some questions he wanted to ask when they did an in-person interview.

"Ooh, perfect!" Heather said. "I took a look when you sent me the link earlier and it does look great. I'm impressed with Leo's work. Especially since he's so young. He's gotta be right out of college."

Nick smiled. "He's twenty-five and graduated a few years ago, but yeah, his work is very impressive."

Heather shot him a sidelong glance. "So I'm curious. Did *you* write the About Me page or did he write it for you?"

Nick shrugged. "It was a collaborative effort. I wrote most of it and he made a few tweaks."

"Well, I love the way it tells a lot about who you are and why you're so passionate about matchmaking."

"Yeah? You think so?"

"Yeah. It was touching. It felt like a nice tribute to Nic."

"Thanks." He smiled and put an arm around his sister, hugging her to his side.

Many of their friends had called him and his wife Nick and Nic. The jokes had gotten ridiculous over the years but sometimes he missed hearing them. It was nice to have Heather refer to her that way.

And, frankly, nice for him to think of Nicole without feeling depressed.

The holidays had felt heavy and dreary since her death. He'd made the mistake of pushing away her brother, Ford, so not only had he lost Nicole, he'd lost a guy he'd viewed as a brother. It had made the holidays a struggle and it was only in the past year that he finally felt like he was starting to come out of the fog of grief.

Now, Nick felt a surge of hope he hadn't experienced in a long time. An excitement about the upcoming season. Thinking about Nicole was a warm, wistful feeling inside of his chest instead of a weight dragging him down.

"Ooh. It looks like the tree lighting is starting." Heather elbowed Nick in the ribs.

Nick turned to see the deputy mayor standing by the stage with Heath Kelly, a former soap actor, Hallmark heartthrob, and the lead in some of their network's latest queer-themed holiday movies.

Heather glanced around and snickered. "It cracks me up the way people go nuts about him. I mean, I guess he's fine. If you're into that."

Nick chuckled. "Yeah, he's not bad." Heath had a thick head of wavy dark hair and chiseled good looks, so he was pretty easy on the eyes.

Nick had always known, *theoretically*, that he found guys attractive but he'd only been eighteen when he'd met Nicole. After an offhand mention to Nicole that he might be bi, Nicole had nodded, smiled, then lovingly pestered him into admitting what type of men he found attractive.

Over the years, she'd made playful little jokes about who his hall pass celebrities would be and they'd found it funny when a few of the men they both listed wound up being the same.

But Nick had never … he'd never *acted* on it. He'd never had the opportunity. He and Nicole had been inseparable from the beginning. Committed. Monogamous.

Since Nicole's death, Nick had gone on a few dates but they'd felt all wrong.

It had been too soon. After the one-year anniversary of her death, everyone had acted like it was time for him to move on and he'd *tried*, but he hadn't been ready. The dates had ended disastrously and he'd vowed he wasn't going to do that again. And for a while now, he'd been so busy setting up the business he'd hardly had time to think about his own social life.

It had been foolish to hope he'd find true love a second time anyway. What he'd had with Nic was one-in-a-lifetime. He'd had his chance at happiness and now, it was his mission to help other people discover that.

Nick glanced over at Leo, watching him laugh at something Hayden said.

Hopefully he'd find someone nice for Leo. He was talented, kind, funny, good-looking … he deserved someone extra special.

A moment later, the audience fell silent and Nick glanced back at the podium to see the mayor step up to the microphone and introduce Heath Kelly.

"I'm so glad to finally be here with you all in Christmas Falls," Heath said, his voice smooth and resonant. "This is such a lovely way to start the season."

The crowd cheered, applauding.

"I know I'm pretty," he joked, "but how about we light this tree and give you something beautiful to see?"

Nick chuckled and exchanged a smile with his sister before he lifted his camera to his eye and zoomed in on the actor.

As Heath continued, Nick captured a few more photos of people in the crowds, only half-listening to the speech. He got a shot of a young child on their parents' shoulders, a couple snuggling, and an older kid with two cookies clutched in their fist and a smear of chocolate on their cheek.

He hesitated when he caught a glimpse of Ford in the crowd, surprised to see him here. He wondered if he should try to approach him. No, probably not. They were both enjoying the event, no point in risking an awkward public situation.

With a sigh, Nick moved on, scanning the crowd for more interesting shots. He got a photo of a woman wearing light-up antlers and a young couple who he'd set up last year holding hands and still looking madly in love.

The crowd's energy swelled as Heath threw the switch and the tree lit up. Everyone cheered as the bright lights lit up the park.

Nick snapped a few more pictures, turning to get shots of the people behind him, capturing the colors playing across their faces.

When Nick's lens stopped on Leo's face, he paused.

Leo laughed at something Hayden said, his skin lit up with shades of blue, red, and green and Nick clicked, taking a handful of shots before he forced himself to turn away.

CHAPTER FOUR

"How do we do this photo thing?" Leo asked, raising an eyebrow at Nick as they met on the sidewalk in front of Ginger's Breads.

Obviously, it was part of Nick's matchmaking service to do portraits of the people who signed up for his services. It was written very clearly on the website.

But something about Nick wanting to photograph *him* made Leo feel all fluttery inside. Which was silly, but well, sometimes, Leo had to admit to himself he could be a ridiculous person. He fell in love easily and got hurt easily. That was how it was. He just had to keep reminding himself Nick was off-limits.

"I thought we'd wander around town," Nick said with a smile. "And I'll get some shots of you as we talk."

"Oh, okay. So more candid pictures than posed?" Leo asked.

"A little of both," Nick said with a shrug. "If that works for you."

"Sure. It's great. I've just never done this before."

"Most of my clients haven't," Nick explained. "So I've developed a system for getting them to relax and show up as their authentic selves. Now, let's head this way."

He tilted his head toward The Snowflake Shack, which sat right next to the bakery.

"So how'd you get into photography?" Leo asked as they strolled past the diner, which wafted out the tempting scents of burgers and fries.

There was graffiti on the wall—part of a social art experiment by some students at U of C last winter—showing children building a snowman while snowflakes, ornaments, and gifts hung in the air above them.

Rather than answer, Nick walked ahead of him and turned back, aiming the camera lens at him and snapping a few photos. Leo tried not to make an awkward face every time he heard the click of the shutter.

"My uncle is a professional photographer and I looked up to him growing up. It's been a hobby for most of my life."

"Very cool. It always looks fun. I just take dumb shots on my phone."

"It is fun. It can get expensive though," Nick said with a rueful chuckle. "There's always some new equipment to buy."

"Now you can write it off as a business expense," Leo joked.

Nick laughed, lowering his camera to grin. "True."

He turned back and fell into step beside Leo again. They

paused at the curb, waiting for traffic to clear before they crossed Blitzen Street.

"How familiar are you with the town?" Nick asked. "Would you like a guided tour?"

Leo was so tempted to lie and say he'd love it but he didn't want to take advantage of Nick's kindness.

"Honestly, I've been visiting regularly since late last winter. At this point, I've eaten in most of the restaurants and checked out most of the shops."

"Oh right, that makes sense. No worries then."

Was it Leo's imagination or did he look a little bit disappointed? *Probably my imagination.*

"So you've been inside Mistletoe Movies?" Nick asked as he did the walk backwards and shoot photos thing again.

"Yeah, it's fun! I mean, I'd never been in a movie shop before—"

Nick groaned. "Thank you for making me feel old."

"Well, you certainly don't look it."

The shutter clicked again, several times in a row, before Nick lowered the camera and shrugged. "Uh, thanks. I guess I'm not doing too bad for nearly forty."

"No, you're hot," Leo blurted out, then promptly wished he could dive through the door of Rudolph's and disappear into the restaurant, never to be seen again.

That wouldn't be weird at all.

"Uhh, thanks." Nick fumbled his camera, nearly dropping it before he lifted it to his face again.

"You're about to back up into traffic, by the way," Leo pointed out.

"Shit." Nick stopped at the edge of the curb, teetering a little. Thankfully, there were no cars going that direction at the moment. "Good catch. I'm usually better at doing two things at once."

Hmm, if you're straight, why are you acting all flustered by the compliment, Mr. Matchmaker?

But no, Leo was probably reading too much into it. Maybe Nick was shy about getting compliments.

"Oh! Have you been in Season's Readings?" Nick asked, speaking quickly, his words tumbling over one another. "We should cross here and walk by it. It's a cute little bookstore. Nicole used to do book signings there and …"

Amused, Leo followed Nick across Christmas Boulevard, then turned right to walk along that side of the street, Nick talking the whole time about Nicole's book signings.

Which, honestly, sounded pretty cool.

Leo listened intently as Nick rambled on while they walked. He paused occasionally so Nick could take some pictures before they started up again. They passed Jolly Java—the cute little café that had changed hands recently—and Tidings & Joy, which was a general store Leo had been in a few times.

Nick seemed to relax again as they did a few staged shots in front of Nutcrackers—a shop with a giant wooden nutcracker outside that Leo pretended to kiss on the cheek in a playful pose—then finally stopped beside Frosty's.

"Okay, I think that's enough," Nick said. "I've got some great shots."

"Yeah?" Leo glanced over.

"Well, you're easy to photograph," Nick said, tucking his camera into a bag and zipping it closed. "Very photogenic."

"Oh, am I?" Leo grinned at him, surprised.

"Yeah. Great cheekbones." Nick turned away, walking toward Frosty's. "Now, c'mon. Let's get that lunch and beer I promised you as thanks for getting the website up and running."

"Tell me what you're looking for in a date," Nick asked twenty minutes later, taking a sip of his beer.

"Umm." Leo squinted at him across the table. "Isn't that why I filled out the questionnaire?"

Nick shrugged. "It's part of the process, yeah, but not all I work with. I like having these one-on-one interviews too. It gives me a better sense of someone's personality and likes or dislikes. Besides, we made a few tweaks based on your suggestions so some of your answers aren't accurate anymore."

"True."

Leo had been surprised when Nick invited him out for a drink after the photoshoot but he'd framed it as a "thanks for getting the website up and running" kinda thing. Not an "I'm going to interrogate you about relationships" one.

Leo's happy mood at the compliment suddenly plummeted. Right. The *interview.*

Nick would set him up with other people soon. Damn it. That sounded less exciting by the moment.

"Okay, so your question is super broad," Leo pointed out. "I mean, what I look for in a date … like the person? The actual going out part? What are you hoping for? I need you to be more specific."

"Fair enough." Nick set his pint glass down, wiping a faint trace of foam from his upper lip. "So tell me what a perfect first date would look like to you. The going out part. Not the person."

"Hmm. Well, I'd want an opportunity to talk to someone a lot," Leo said slowly, reaching for a pretzel to dunk in the warm beer cheese dip they'd ordered to share.

"So definitely not a movie or a show where you had to be quiet and just watch?" Nick asked.

"Right, exactly. I mean, it's fine later on once I know the person. But for a first date? No way. You don't have the opportunity to have much of a conversation."

"Makes sense."

"Meeting for coffee is good. Brunch, lunch, dinner are all good. Or something more active." His expression brightened. "Honestly, most of the Christmas Festival stuff sounds *perfect.*"

"Which ones would you definitely want to do?"

"Umm, the holiday cocktail hour sounds great. The cooking class could be fun too or the wine tasting. I'd enjoy that."

"How do you feel about crafts?"

Leo shrugged. "I'd be up for trying them but I'm not like … super crafty or anything."

"Noted."

Leo glanced at him. "Do you keep all this in your head?"

"Yes?" Nick looked a little sheepish. "Why? Should I be taking actual notes?"

"I mean … I'd never remember everything but if it works for you, why change it?" Leo shrugged. He thought it was cute Nick wanted his opinion.

"For now it works," Nick said, reaching for his glass. "We'll see if it changes now that I have more people to keep track of."

Leo laughed, pleased Nick had already seen an uptick in signups for his services in the past few days.

"So what about the caroling?" Nick asked.

Leo snickered. "It sounds fun to watch but no one wants to hear me sing. I sound like a bag of cats being tortured."

"No cat torturing, got it," Nick said with a grin. "Jelly will appreciate that."

"Jelly?" Leo shot Nick a quizzical look.

"Oh, uh, my cat."

Leo suppressed a laugh. "You have a cat named Jelly?"

Nick's face went soft. "Her name was Lily when Nicole and I got her but the first morning we had her, she jumped on the table and stuck her whole face in the jar of jelly. It stuck."

"Her face or the nickname?" Leo asked with a chuckle.

"Both. Though, thankfully, she wasn't hurt."

"Good!" Leo leaned in. "Have any pictures?"

"Of that incident? No."

"Of the cat in general," Leo clarified.

"Oh, yes." Nick sat back, reaching into his pocket for his phone. The gesture showed off the long line of his body and the way his light gray sweater clung to his chest and stomach.

Don't be a creep, Leo reminded himself. *He's straight. He's a grieving widow. Don't make it weird, dude!*

To distract himself, Leo focused on the food in front of him, snagging a rosemary fry. God, it was *so good*. He could eat a whole basket of them if he wasn't paying attention.

"Here's Jelly." Nick held out his phone and Leo took it.

"Aww, look at that face! She—" He glanced up questioningly and Nick nodded. "She's adorable!"

"Yeah, she knows it too," Nick said, but there was a fondness in his tone he didn't even try to hide.

Leo handed the phone back, their fingers brushing.

"So, you like pets?" Nick said, clearing his throat.

"Yeah, I love animals," Leo said, brightening. "I grew up on a farm."

"Really?" Nick looked surprised. "So you're not originally from Chicago?"

"Ha. No. Not even close. My parents have a dairy farm in Wisconsin."

"Yeah?"

"Yep. They have about three hundred Jersey cows and sell milk, cheese, and other dairy products."

"I have to admit, I have no idea what a Jersey cow is."

"It's the breed."

Nick laughed. "I figured *that* much. I just mean I don't know what they look like. Are they the big black and white ones?"

"No, those are Holsteins. Jerseys are smaller. They're a soft brown color with big eyes and dark noses. Very cute." Leo pulled his phone out and pulled up some pictures of the farm he'd taken the last time he was home.

He held the device out to Nick. "Swipe to the right to see more. I promise, none of my naughty pictures are in that folder."

Nick coughed, setting down his beer and pounded his fist against his chest. "Good to know."

He took the phone and swiped through the photos, his eyes crinkling as he stared at them. "Aww, they are cute. Can you pet them?"

"Sure," Leo said, amused. "We pet them all of the time. I mean, they're livestock but we do bond with them. Not me so much anymore, but when I grew up, I helped raise them from the moment they were born until they were retired as milkers."

"But you didn't want to become a farmer for a profession?" Nick asked, handing the phone back.

Leo chuckled. "Not so much. I like going home and being on the farm and helping out but it's not my passion. Not the way it is for my parents or my older brothers Adam and Jason."

"So how'd you get into web development?"

"When I was in high school, Fenner Dairy needed a new website," he said with a laugh. "My parents were trying to build one and if you thought *you* were bad at it, they were a thousand times worse."

"Hey!" Nick protested, but he was laughing too.

"So I watched a bunch of tutorials and pulled something together. It wasn't the best, but it was a place people could contact them and learn about the farm and what products they offer. I've updated it a couple of times since then and I'm extremely happy with it now."

"Cool. I'll have to check it out sometime. Are your parents happy with your career?"

"Oh, yeah, they're super proud of me," Leo said. "It helps that Adam and Jason are there to carry on the farm but we all knew it wasn't the right life for me. Don't get me wrong, there are gay dairy farmers in Wisconsin too, but it isn't the easiest way to meet people, you know?"

"Yeah, I would imagine," Nick said, taking a sip of his beer. "So, this is great, I think I have a few ideas of who I could match you with."

"Okay," Leo said, surprised by the sudden shift in conversation. "Wow, you move fast."

Nick shrugged. "Well, you said you thought some of the festival events would be perfect for dates and a ton are coming up that I want to take advantage of. I'll speak to the guys I have in mind and see what their availability is. Do you have any days in the next few weeks that are booked?"

"Not really," Leo said with a little hum, checking his calendar on his phone. "I'm generally done with work around five or six in the evening on weekdays but I can be a little flexible if I need to be. Oh, I'm doing Thanksgiving with Hayden and Joel next Thursday. Otherwise, my schedule is pretty clear, to be honest."

"Perfect!" Nick beamed, holding up his glass. "Here's to finding you the perfect date!"

Leo clinked. "Here's hoping!"

CHAPTER FIVE

"You don't like Christmas," Leo said, completely flabbergasted as he turned to look at bachelor number one the following night.

They'd just walked into the arts and crafts holiday fair being held inside the Christmas Falls Festival Museum and, well … that seemed a *little* weird to Leo.

His date, Mike, shrugged. "Nah, I mean it's just an over-commercialized event. Totally pointless except as an excuse to drive fourth quarter sales."

"It *can* be," Leo said slowly as they approached the first table at the craft market. "I mean, I've definitely seen people fall into the trap of focusing all on the buying gifts part of the celebration and ignoring the rest, but you've got to admit it can be more than that."

Mike made a face. "Commercialism is still at the heart of it."

"It doesn't have to be," Leo pointed out. "What about spending time with family?"

"Which adds more pressure to buy, buy, buy," Mike said, stuffing his hands into his jacket pockets.

One of the vendors at a table frowned at them and Leo made a mental note to go back and shop at their booth when he wasn't walking around with a total wet blanket of a guy.

Leo thought of some Christmases he'd had as a kid with only a few presents under the tree when milk prices were down and his family struggled. And sure, at the time, he'd been bummed he hadn't gotten the latest and greatest piece of technology all of the kids in school were clamoring for.

But he still had great memories.

"I think it can be special even without a ton of gifts," Leo said earnestly. "I mean, my family always had a lot of fun traditions. We went for drives to see the lights, decorate the Christmas tree together, listen to music—"

"See!" Mike said triumphantly. "All steeped in commercialism. People have to pay for the car and gas and the lights and electricity. They have to buy a tree and ornaments they use once a year. And the music! That costs money too. Plus, whatever you play it on."

He looked proud for having torn apart Leo's most treasured memories and reduced them to commodities.

Leo was tempted to point out they'd cut down trees they'd grown on their own farm, many of the ornaments had been handed down through several generations, and they'd listened to records from Leo's grandparents' collection on a vintage turntable belonging to Leo's grandparents but he had a feeling Mike wouldn't be impressed.

"Well," Leo said as diplomatically as he could manage. "I

can see why it wouldn't be for everyone. What made you choose to live in Christmas Falls then?"

Seemed like a *super* weird decision for a guy who hated the holiday.

Mike blinked. "I grew up here."

"And you never thought about moving elsewhere?" Leo prompted.

"No."

Wow. This guy sure was … something.

Leo spotted a booth with some hand-carved gnomes his mom would like and he felt a flash of irritation that he now felt awkward about going over to pick one out for her.

Thanks, Mike.

He was definitely coming back another night though to get one.

Gah, why couldn't Mike see giving gifts could be *joyful* too. Leo loved supporting local artisans and finding a present he knew the recipient would love. There was nothing like watching someone's face light up with joy at the sight of a gift they adored.

But hey, the night wasn't over yet. Maybe there was a way to salvage it. Leo cleared his throat. "So, why did you choose to come to this event?"

Mike shrugged. "There was nothing else to do. And I wanted to meet you."

"Yeah?" Leo asked. The latter part of the statement was flattering but getting excited about *that* felt like grasping at straws. Even for him. "What made you decide to sign up for a matchmaking service?"

Mike shrugged again. "I didn't have much luck meeting people otherwise."

You don't say, Leo thought drily. *Can't imagine why. Could it be your attitude toward everything?*

But hey, Nick had recommended the guy so there had to be *something* redeeming about him.

Unfortunately, try as Leo might, the night didn't improve from there.

While they strolled past the cheerfully decorated booths filled with hopeful vendors eager to make a sale, Leo made vain attempts to spark any conversation to build a connection with Mike.

He mentioned music, movies, TV shows, vacations, work … every single topic he could dredge up but most of Mike's answers were short and ended the conversation before it began. The *only* thing Mike seemed to get fired up about were his rants on commercialism, which included Leo's role in helping companies set up websites to market shit people didn't need.

Which, fine, Leo could respect up to a certain point but as Mike described his future dream of selling his belongings, buying a used van, and converting it to live off-grid, Leo decided they definitely were *not* a match.

Mindful spending and avoiding overconsumption he could get on board with but there was no way in hell he'd ever be okay with a *toilet* in his kitchen. Nope. No way. Fuck that shit.

Leo edged his way toward the exit, grateful when he finally escaped the crush of bodies in the museum. Outside, the temperature had dropped and Leo rubbed his arms to keep warm as Mike blathered on about some online video he'd watched about van conversion.

"Well," Leo said brightly when there was the barest hint of a break in the conversation. "Would you look at the time? I have a big workday tomorrow so I think I'll have to let you go!"

Mike looked crestfallen. "Oh no. I was having a nice time too."

Leo tried not to grimace. That made one of them.

"I'll, uh, see you around then?" Leo said, edging toward the street.

Mike shook his head. "Oh, no. I'll walk you to your door like a gentleman. You live over the bakery, right? It's on my way."

Damn it. Leo regretted telling Mike that earlier but, in his defense, he'd been desperate for *something* to discuss.

"Oh, that's, um, very sweet but *really* not necessary," he said hastily.

"No, I insist!"

Leo gritted his teeth and turned in that direction.

Thankfully, the walk to Leo's apartment was nearly silent and he spent most of it enjoying the crispness of the late fall air and the crunch of leaves under his feet. He couldn't *wait* for the first snow.

"Romantic night, isn't it?" Mike asked as they passed the dumpster in the parking lot behind Ginger's Breads.

"Mmm," Leo said. The smell of old food and cooking oil didn't really do it for him but hey, to each his own.

Though Leo was sure he would have ignored the ick and found it romantic if he was out with someone he clicked with … someone like Nick …

"So, when can I take you out again?" Mike asked when they reached the back door.

Leo already had his keys in his hand and he quickly fumbled for the correct one.

"Umm." Leo smiled tightly as he glanced at Mike. Well, this was awkward as fuck. "That's sweet but I am not sure we're a great fit."

An offended look crossed Mike's face. "Why not? What's wrong with me?"

So many things, Leo thought but that was unkind. He was probably perfect for someone out there. Just not Leo.

"Uhh, it's not you!" he said hastily as he jabbed the key into the lock and twisted. "It's, um, me?"

"Oh right," Mike said, scoffing. "That's what *everyone* says. C'mon. We should see if we have some chemistry."

He leaned in like he planned to kiss Leo, eyes closed, lips puckered.

"I can't go to the bathroom where my food is cooked!" Leo blurted out, fumbling for the knob and throwing himself inside the building. "Sorry! Good luck!"

Jelly wound around Nick's ankles and mewed for food as he opened the dishwasher and loaded in the dirty bowl and spoon from the pumpkin cheesecake ice cream he'd eaten while watching TV earlier.

He'd yawned his way through the latest episode of *Northdale Heights*, then finally decided to head to bed. He'd been half-asleep on the couch anyway.

Jelly gave a particularly strident meow.

"Yeesh. Give me a minute, cat." His phone vibrated in his pocket.

Hmm. Probably a marketing text or something. He'd check it when he got upstairs though to be sure it wasn't important.

Nick tossed in a cleaning tablet, closed the dishwasher, then pressed *Start*.

He poured a little kibble into Jelly's dish, turned out the kitchen lights except for the one over the stove, then checked that the doors were locked.

Even now, it was his least favorite time of day.

He hated how quiet the house was, how empty it felt as he trudged up to his bedroom, knowing he'd be slipping into the wide bed alone. He felt the familiar pang of missing Nicole, wishing he'd walk into the bedroom and find her cozied up in bed, nose buried in a book.

Even the company of Jelly, who would be up as soon as she was done with her snack, didn't soothe that ache.

Nick was halfway through brushing his teeth when his phone buzzed again and he remembered he was supposed to check it. *Hmm.* Maybe Leo was onto something with the suggestion to write more down …

The first text was from some random company but, to Nick's surprise, the second was from Leo.

Bad news. Date #1 was a dud.

Nick frowned around the toothbrush and responded, ***Sorry! Unfortunately, they're not all winners right off the bat!***

Although he'd had a few couples who had hit it off immediately and quickly moved in together or got married.

I know. But like ... this was tragically awful Nick.

Concerned, Nick spat out the toothpaste, then wiped his mouth on the nearby hand towel.

Was he a creep or a jerk or something? Because I'll let him go as a client if he crossed a line.

Oh no! Leo fired back. ***God, not like that. He was polite, I guess? Leaned in for a kiss when I very much was not feeling it but otherwise, a decent guy. We have very different values, I think.***

Hmm, in what way?

Uhh, can I call? I think it would be easier to explain.

Sure. Give me ten?

No prob. Call me when you're ready.

Nick finished getting ready for bed, trotted down the stairs to grab a notepad, pen, and earbuds, then went back up to his bedroom.

Jelly followed on his heels, clearly confused about the change in her human's routine.

In a pair of plaid pajama pants and a white tee, Nick slid under the covers and got his earbuds connected.

He called Leo, who picked up quickly.

"Okay, so I feel bad if I made Mike sound like he was a creep," he said the moment the phone connected. "He's not. A little weird but, like, he politely walked me to my door and asked me out on another date."

"If he tried to kiss you and you didn't want it, that *was* creepy," Nick pointed out, frowning.

"Maybe gently remind him unless people are really giving off interested vibes, he should ask instead of trying to initiate?" Leo said.

"I can definitely do that," Nick assured him. "And seriously if he does it again, I'm booting him out. I don't want you to have to deal with stuff like that. I mean, no one should."

Leo was silent for a moment. "Yeah, thanks."

"So, uh," Nick cleared his throat. "Even before that, you didn't feel there was a good connection?"

Leo chuckled. "Yeah, no. Not so much. Mike, uh, has strong feelings about commercialism. And like … fine. Whatever. But he insulted my career and hates Christmas. Which made the event very awkward."

Nick winced and scribbled down, *Ask clients about views on holidays.*

Jelly jumped up on the bed, landing beside Nick's feet. She walked closer to his hand, bumping it with her head and he patted her, enjoying the purr she immediately let out, before picking up his pen again and jotting down a few more thoughts.

"Nick?" Leo said a moment later. "You still there?"

"Yeah, sorry," he said, distracted. "I'm taking notes."

"Aww, you listened to my advice," Leo teased.

"Sure, why wouldn't I?" Nick asked, perplexed.

"I dunno. Didn't expect it, I suppose."

"I'm open to change," Nick explained as Jelly hopped onto his thigh. "I never want to get so stuck in my ways I become inflexible."

"That's a good trait to have," Leo said warmly. "Maybe make a note to ask your clients that too. See if they like change or prefer routine."

"Great suggestion!" Nick jotted it below the other notes with his right hand as he tried to pat Jelly with his left. "Man, having you as my test client is incredibly helpful."

"Glad I could be of service," Leo teased. "So what are you up to tonight?"

"Well," Nick said drily. "My night is less exciting than yours, I think. I watched TV—"

"Ooh, what'd you watch?" Leo asked.

Nick chuckled and capped the pen, tossing it and the notepad aside.

"*Northdale Heights*," he admitted.

"That's so good! I can't believe I missed the latest episode for a date with Mike the Grouch."

"Well, I won't spoil it for you then," Nick said, chuckling when Jelly bumped his chin.

"What's so funny?" Leo asked.

"Oh, the cat. She won't let me be. Has to be in the middle of absolutely *everything*."

"I'm surprised I didn't see her when I was over."

"There's a reason I lock her out of my office. Also, I'm afraid she'll bolt out the other door and go for an adventure in the backyard when I have clients over."

"Yeah, fair," Leo said. It sounded like he was smiling. "Should I leave you to spend time with her?"

"Uhh," Nick said, feeling strangely reluctant to hang up. "I mean, she is used to our cuddles before bed but I can talk more unless you're in a hurry."

"Nah. I'm winding down before bed too." Leo let out a wistful sigh. "Cuddles sound nice though."

"Well, I'll keep looking for your future cuddle partner," Nick promised him. "I have another guy in mind for you all lined up."

"Yeah, okay," Leo said. "So, umm, message me with the details whenever. Thanks, Nick. Goodnight."

He was gone before Nick could even respond and he stared at his phone for a moment, confused by the abrupt ending to their conversation.

"Well, that was strange, Jelly Belly," he said with a sigh as he plugged his phone in.

The cat bumped her head against his chin again in solidarity.

Nick set the pen and the notepad aside, smiling a little wistfully at the logo at the top of the page. Flowery script said, *From the Desk of Morgan Nicola*.

Which was Nicole's pen name.

"Cuddles before bed do sound nice," Nick admitted aloud. It was what he missed more than anything, really.

He turned out the light and settled on the bed, letting Jelly curl up beside him, pushing her head into his palm for more petting. His feline companion would have to do.

"Night, Jelly Roll," he said with a sigh, closing his eyes.

But other than the rumble of the cat's purr, there was no answer.

CHAPTER SIX

The White Elephant Pub was a little more upscale than Frosty's. It had wood-paneled walls, cozy tables, secluded booths around the exterior, and there were tasteful Christmas lights twined with pine garland strung everywhere.

The pub was closed to the public for the event and tables had been rearranged into a half-moon shape, with different bottles of wine set up.

Leo walked over to the main table, smiling at the woman behind it.

She smiled back. "Good evening. Welcome to The White Elephant. You're here for the wine tasting?"

"Yes," Leo said, handing over his ID. "Leo Fenner. I should be on the list. I prepaid."

She scanned a list then marked off his name. "Yes, you're all set. Let me tell you how it works. You will get six tastes, which you can mark off on this card here—along with your impression and a score of each wine."

"Perfect."

She smiled at him. "My name is Elaine, by the way. Let me know if you have any questions. I'll be here all evening."

"Thanks, Elaine." Leo leaned in. "Actually. I'm, uh, meeting a date. Guy about my age named Andrew. Do you know if he's here yet?"

"Oh. Well, I believe he's already here by the bar. He's dressed in, uh, red and green."

"Thanks! That's helpful." Leo had seen pictures of Andrew before but he didn't want to make an ass of himself by approaching the wrong person.

"You can hang your coat over there," Elaine said, gesturing towards the rack they'd set up in the corner. "And feel free to start wherever, though the tables are arranged from light whites to medium whites to more light-bodied reds and finally, at the end there, the more full-bodied reds."

After Leo hung up his coat and grabbed a wine glass, he surveyed the crowd of people milling around talking.

They all appeared to be paired-off couples, a small group of thirty-year-old women, and, as he edged his way closer to the bar … an elf, standing by himself dressed in red and green.

Oh no.

The elf's face lit up. "Hi there, Leo! I'm Twinkle Toes!" he said cheerfully as he held out a hand.

Leo shook, blinking. "Uh, I thought it was Andrew Mulford?"

"Not while the festival is on!" He jiggled his head and the tiny bells on his hat chimed.

"Until then, I'm Santa's helper!"

"Oh are you uh, volunteering?" Leo asked, grasping at straws. Maybe he'd come straight from working some festival event requiring him to dress as an elf and he was still in character.

"Nope, just trying to get in the mood!" Andrew winked.

Oh boy, here we go. Date number two was off to a roaring start.

No, give the guy a chance, Leo sternly reminded himself. *No need to be rude. Maybe he's … a little quirky. He's probably perfectly nice, even though his voice is annoyingly nasal.*

It had been days but Leo could still hear the sound of Nick's low chuckle in his ear … God, he had a *great* voice.

But Nick doesn't want you, Leo reminded himself. *He's a nice human being. You need to focus on the guys who are* actually *interested in dating you. Like this elf-dude.*

"Great to meet you, um, Twinkle Toes," Leo said, pasting a smile onto his face. He would make the best of this night if it killed him. "So, um, I've done a few wine tastings before. How about you?"

"Nope! Should be fun though." Andrew did an excited little wiggle, making his bells jingle again.

"It'll definitely be something," Leo agreed with a sigh.

They made awkward small talk for a few minutes before Leo said, "Do you want to start the tasting? I think we're supposed to help ourselves."

He gestured to the tables where people had begun sampling the wines.

"Sure!" Andrew smiled and Leo let go of a little of the tension inside him.

Okay, so the elf shtick was a little … off-putting but he *was* good-looking, with dark eyes and a nice mouth. Leo needed to give the guy a fair shot.

"Hey now, did you sneak in here, Harold?" one of the servers teased as they passed by, giving a nearby man who had to be in his eighties a pointed look. "We all know you're too young to be drinking!"

Harold grinned and said something back Leo couldn't hear. It made Leo smile. He loved how friendly everyone in town was.

"So, tell me about yourself," Leo said as he and Andrew got in line to sample the wines at the first table.

Andrew lit up. "Oh, well, I work for a bank."

"You're not a loan officer, are you?" Leo asked, thinking of Nick.

A puzzled look crossed Andrew's face. "No, why do you ask?"

"Uh, no reason. So, how do you like it?"

"It's great! My favorite is when dogs come through the drive-through. I keep dog biscuits on hand for them."

Leo laughed, a little more of the earlier tension slipping away. "That *does* sound fun."

"What do you enjoy doing for a hobby?" Leo asked.

He tried to listen attentively while Andrew talked about his love of Christmas and the way he started preparing six months ahead of time but it was a little overwhelming. He could hardly keep up with the excited babble about hand-calligraphed Christmas cards begun in June.

Nor did Leo care, to be honest.

Thankfully, they reached the front of the line. Leo read the placard describing the crémant style.

"Ooh. Sounds interesting," he said, eager to try it. He helped himself to a small sample of the wine.

He carefully sniffed it, then took a small sip. "Yeah, that's nice. What do you think?"

He glanced over to see Andrew had already downed his. Geeze, that was concerning. But maybe he was thirsty? Or nervous? Yeah, maybe he was nervous. Besides, he had said he'd never done a tasting before.

Maybe he didn't know he needed to sip slowly and savor it. And, uh, pace himself.

"Ehh, it's okay," Andrew said with a shrug, his bells jingling again. "I can think of better things to put in my mouth though."

Leo froze, wondering if that was a come-on. But no, Andrew was reaching for the bottle of Prosecco. *Surely* that's what he meant.

"This is interesting. I've never seen a tasting set up this way before," Leo commented. It had certainly never been like this in Chicago, anyway.

Andrew grunted and splashed another healthy amount into his glass. Leo caught a glimpse of Elaine eyeing him from a few feet away, a disapproving expression on her face.

Whoops, hopefully she hadn't overheard him. The setup was fine. Just different.

"So, um, tell me about your holiday decorations, Andrew," Leo said desperately. "If you love Christmas, you must go all out for those."

Andrew pressed close, his chest bumping against Leo's arm.

Leo shifted a little bit to the right. Hopefully Andrew would take the hint he'd encroached on Leo's personal space.

"Yes," Andrew said, smiling. "I have over three thousand lights on my house."

"Wow, you're pretty much Clark Griswold then." Leo joked.

Andrew's expression hardened. "I hate that movie."

"Oh." Leo blinked and reached for the bottle of cava. "I'm sorry?"

"It's okay. You can make it up to me later." His hand grazed the side of Leo's thigh.

"Wow, it's uh, crowded in here, huh?" Leo said, fanning himself with the tasting notes card. "It's getting warm."

"I can think of better ways to heat you up," Andrew murmured and, for a moment, Leo was sure he'd misheard.

"What?"

"I said, I can think of better ways to heat you up," Andrew said, so close now his lips tickled Leo's ear.

What the hell?

"Uhh, well, it seems a little bit too soon for that," Leo said with an awkward laugh as he set down his glass. "Let's uh, let's fill out our tasting notes!"

He waved the paper and reached for a nearby pencil. But when he bent over to write his notes, Andrew's hand grazed his ass. Then *pinched*.

Leo yelped. "Um, so I think we're supposed to be mingling and talking to other people about the wine too!" he said, backing away. "Back in a bit!"

It was true. Plenty of people were standing around talking as they sipped their wine and Leo gratefully escaped into the crowd.

He breathed a little easier when he was surrounded by the women he'd spotted earlier.

"I feel like the crémant is a little sharp," one of them said.

Leo nodded. "Yes. Me too. The Prosecco is nice though."

"It is," another woman said, her gaze warm, and Leo stuck out his hand.

"Hi, sorry to crash your conversation. I'm Leo Fenner, by the way."

"Stephanie."

After she introduced herself, everyone else chimed in too, welcoming him to town.

Unfortunately, it wasn't long before the women disappeared toward the table marked 'light whites' and Leo reluctantly returned to his date who had moved on to the table of reds.

"I don't know why you ran away like that but, God, I couldn't stop staring at your ass in those pants the whole time," Andrew said, leering at him. "So fucking hot."

"Uhh, thanks?" Leo said. Fuck, they'd only started to try the wines so far. This would be a painfully long evening. He read the card on the first wine aloud. "A red blend, which has notes of toasted vanilla and marshmallow over jammy dark fruits …"

Leo poured himself a small mouthful, sipped it, then brightened. "Ooh this is nice," he said.

Andrew leaned in. "You know what would be even nicer?"

"Nope and I don't want to know," Leo said, slipping away. "Gonna go mingle again."

He fled for the safety of the women again. Stephanie gave him a sympathetic smile. "Date not going so well?"

"How'd you guess?" he asked grimly.

She giggled. "Well, we'll protect you."

Leo grinned. The date might be terrible, but he'd met some nice people from Christmas Falls, so it wasn't all bad.

He tried not to stare enviously at a couple nearby who'd been flirting through the whole tasting. He was pretty sure one of them was named Rocco and that he'd bought Jolly Java from the previous owners and the other one was the deputy mayor, though his name escaped Leo at the moment.

At least *someone's* date was going well tonight.

"Okay, you can do this," he muttered, psyching himself up for another round with Twinkle Toes. He'd have to be firm and let Andrew know he'd come on way too strong.

Reluctantly, he returned to the table for another sample of wine.

According to the placard, it was, "a cabernet sauvignon with hints of spiced plum and woodsmoke."

"You seem kinda tense," Andrew said as Leo lifted his glass to his mouth. "You should come with me after this and I can give you a massage. I have this candy cane flavored lotion I can rub all over you and—"

Leo turned and looked at him, mouth agape. "I am *tense* because you're creeping me out," he whispered furiously. "I can overlook the elf thing but—"

"The elf thing is important to me!"

"I'm sorry." Leo grimaced. "I'm not trying to insult your … thing. It's—"

"You are *very* rude," Andrew huffed. "I'm only trying to show you a nice time."

"I wouldn't call making weird comments a nice time," Leo pointed out. "You're crossing a line."

Andrew sniffed. "And here I was going to invite you to come home with me and introduce you to the North Pole."

Leo blinked.

There was a chance Andrew called his house the North Pole but Leo had a horrible, horrible feeling he referred to something else entirely.

"I'm not interested," Leo said stiffly.

Andrew threw back his glass of wine and stood. "Fine! I'll go find someone else to jingle my bells."

Leo stifled the urge to scream and bang his head against the nearest flat surface.

Striiiiiiike two.

"And this is my co-worker, Alannah." Smiling, Heather introduced the last person at the friends' Thanksgiving dinner party. "Lana, this is my brother Nick."

Nick held out a hand. "Nice to meet you, Alannah."

"Lovely to meet you too, Nick," Alannah said. She had a low, slightly husky voice, and her gaze was warm as she shook. "I've heard so much about you."

There was something in the way she looked at Nick that gave him a sudden, sinking suspicion about where this was going. It was painfully obvious he and Alannah were the only single people in the group. Everyone else who'd been invited was coupled up.

Hell, he'd set up two of the couples there!

Nick glanced over to see his sister disappearing through the crowd in her living room and stifled a sigh. Huh. Apparently, matchmaking ran in the family.

He turned back to Alannah, not wanting to be rude. "So, you're a teacher?"

"Librarian."

"Oh, nice. Does that get challenging with some of the recent book banning?"

She gave him a rueful smile. "Well, thankfully, we haven't had any issues in this community, but yeah, I have some friends from the library sciences program we were in who are dealing with it."

Thankfully, that conversation carried them through enjoying the appetizers set out on the buffet. As they ate, they were both drawn into a discussion about the local school board and Nick honestly didn't mind when he was seated next to Alannah at dinner.

She was a lovely woman. Easy on the eyes *and* easy to talk to. He could see them becoming friends.

The problem was, he didn't feel a spark of anything else.

Hmm. Speaking of dating, he wondered how Leo was doing on his date tonight. Hopefully it was going better than it had with Mike.

God, Nick had missed the mark there. Mike had pets and had said he was looking for the same things Leo was. He was interested in a monogamous, long-term relationship. He wanted to get married someday and have children. He'd talked about wanting to travel, another interest Leo had …

But the personality had been a serious mismatch, apparently. Nick had no idea Mike was so-anti Christmas.

At least the guy Leo was on a date with tonight was pro-Christmas.

Andrew's voice was a little grating but he seemed like a great guy. Very well put together and he'd spoken warmly about pets and the holidays and looking for someone to make his holidays merry and bright.

That would be good for Leo!

Nick reached for his phone, wondering if Leo had sent an update. *Hmm. Nope. Nothing.*

Nick pushed away the flicker of disappointment. That was a good sign!

"Nick?" Alannah asked softly. "Could you pass the mashed

potatoes? I'm getting full but I can't resist a second helping of them."

"Oh, sure," he said, sliding his phone back into his pocket with one hand while he reached for the bowl with the other. They were going fast and he was glad. The recipe was always a huge hit whenever he served them.

"These are seriously so good," she raved as she scooped some onto her plate. "You like to cook then?"

Nick smiled. "I do. I didn't at first but I had to learn."

"After your wife died?"

Nick flinched, though he was sure she didn't mean it to be cruel. "Ahh, no. I got more serious about cooking shortly after she started writing."

"I'm sorry." She touched his arm. "I didn't mean to bring up a bad memory."

"No, not at all," he said with a quiet laugh. "You're fine."

Alannah frowned. "So, you walked in with the mashed potatoes already made. I thought they had to be made fresh? They never turn out as good when I reheat them."

Relieved at the change of subject, Nick smiled. "The secret is to make them a day or two ahead. Then about three or four hours before you want to serve them, you stick them in a slow cooker on low. They turn out *perfectly* when you reheat slowly with the lid on."

"You must add something though," she said with a small frown. "More milk?"

"Nope. Just don't take the lid off or stir until they're totally hot. That's the trick."

"Huh, well, I'm impressed. Handsome, he can cook, *and* he's a matchmaker." She shot him a flirty smile and he tried not to sigh.

Nope, not a single spark. What the hell was wrong with him? Other than knowing no one would ever be Nicole.

Nick's phone buzzed in his pocket and he gratefully pulled it out again. He was surprised to see Leo calling though, and frowned.

"Excuse me," he said, slipping back from the table and his empty plate. "I need to take this call. I'll be back shortly."

Several people around him nodded, including Alannah, but Heather shot him a worried glance.

The long dining table took up most of Heather and Edie's dining room and stuck out into the living room. Nick skirted around the end, then slipped out the patio doors onto the deck.

The air was crisp and cool as he stepped outside and he shivered at the late fall temperature.

Leo's call had ended, but Nick called him back. It rang several times before he picked up.

"Sorry, had to go outside before I could answer. I'm at a party," Nick explained.

"Shit, sorry. We can talk later if you want."

Nick chuckled. "It's okay. How's the date going? Or is this call the indication the answer is not well?"

"It was terrible!" Leo said with a sigh. "He's … yeah, I don't even know where to start."

"Oh no," Nick said, frowning. "I am so sorry. What's going on?"

"We can talk later. Honestly, you should enjoy your party. I didn't mean to interrupt."

"Really, it's fine," Nick assured him, leaning against the railing. "It's a low-key friends' Thanksgiving at my sister's place."

"Aww, that sounds fun. Is it like a potluck or …"

"Yeah. Heather and Edie cook a leg of lamb every year and everyone else brings the rest."

"Lamb, huh? Very traditional for Thanksgiving."

Nick laughed. "Well, they have two turkeys on Thanksgiving Day because of going to their respective in-laws' places, so I think they wanted a break."

"Fair. What'd you bring?"

"Smashed potatoes with rosemary brown-butter."

Leo made a pornographic noise. "Oh my God, that sounds amazing."

"They're pretty good if I do say so myself," Nick admitted. "I took a cooking class a few years back and kinda tweaked the recipe I learned in that."

"That's so cool. What made you want to learn to cook?"

He smiled. "Well, Nicole was very *focused* when she was immersed in a story. Especially toward the end of a book, she'd disappear into that world and only surface when it was done. She'd forget to eat, honestly. We eventually figured out it was best if I took care of feeding us both when she was in that mode. I took a cooking class and really enjoyed it."

"Aww, that's sweet," Leo said. "I love how supportive of her career you were."

"We supported each other," Nick explained. "She always took a break for a couple of weeks after finishing each book to focus on us and our relationship. Little date nights and quality time, you know? And when she wasn't in the thick of it, we both shared the household duties pretty evenly. We learned to work with the rhythms of her schedule and once we did, it was perfect for us."

His breath caught a little, remembering how lost he'd felt after she was gone.

"That sounds like an amazing relationship," Leo said and the wistfulness in his tone made Nick feel a little guilty he was talking about the love he'd found instead of focusing on the person he was supposed to be finding for Leo.

"It was," Nick agreed. "But I want to think about *your* relationship now. Tell me about your date tonight."

"So … he showed up in an elf costume."

"Umm," Nick said because that was a little weird. Andrew had been dressed normally when they'd had their one-on-one meeting. Khakis and a polo shirt had seemed perfectly appropriate.

"I thought he'd been volunteering or something, but no. He said he 'wanted to get in the mood' and I was scared to ask if he meant for the holiday event or if this was a kink of his."

Nick snorted. "Leo!"

"Seriously. The way he talked about it … Yikes."

"So, possible elf fetish," Nick said with a frown because he'd totally missed that. "Was that all?"

"That's plenty all on its own," Leo pointed out, though it sounded like he was smiling. "But no. He had nothing to talk about *except* the holidays."

"At least he doesn't hate them?" Nick offered, going for optimism.

Leo let out a little huff. "Yeah, that was a nice change of pace but uh, all of his pets are named after reindeer. He also said his car always has those silly reindeer antlers and nose on it."

"Are we sure he doesn't have a reindeer fetish?" Nick teased.

"Nick!"

"I'm sorry," Nick said, laughing. "I do feel bad, but you have to admit, it's a little bit funny."

"Well, ha-ha, but I'm 0-2 on dates so far. Seriously, this was *so* bad. He said he sends out hand-calligraphed Christmas cards he starts writing in June! Celebrating Christmas is great but I need someone who has interests in something else too!"

"I get that," Nick said. "I thought—I hoped it would be a good change of pace from the first guy. And I swear, none of this came up in the interview."

"Suuure," Leo said with a snort. "Likely story."

"I *promise*. Was there anything else?"

Leo sighed. "Unlike Mike, Andrew was creepy. He kept trying to hit on me and made some joke about introducing me to his North Pole."

"Oh God, Leo, I am so sorry. I did not get those vibes from him at all."

"This is not the man for me and I'm a little concerned you couldn't tell. I thought you were good at your job, Nick!" Leo teased.

"I am!" Nick protested, though he couldn't stop laughing. Thankfully Leo seemed more amused than genuinely upset about the way the night had gone.

The whole situation was *weird* though. He had such a good record matching people up. Okay, so he hadn't had a lot of luck finding anyone for Jett Davis yet, but otherwise he had a great track record. He was used to clients giving him feedback and saying the date was mediocre or there wasn't good chemistry but with Leo it seemed like he was getting it all wrong. "I'm just … not having a lot of luck for you yet," he admitted.

Leo huffed. "Thanks. Good to know I'm the problem."

"No! It wasn't an insult to you," Nick said, growing more serious. "I swear! I was *trying* to find you someone who was enthusiastic about Christmas. I guess I overcorrected."

"Nick, the man was dressed as a fucking elf and he talked about wanting his bells jingled. On a first date!"

"Didn't Hayden dress as an elf last Christmas when he serenaded Joel in front of the bakery?" Nick teased, trying to hide the amusement in his voice and failing utterly.

"Yes, but that was *not* their first date."

"Okay, fair," Nick admitted. "No elf costumes next time. Got it."

"Are you taking notes again?" Leo shot back.

"No. I didn't bring any pen or paper with me. Remember, I'm at a party."

"Shit, sorry!" Leo said. "I honestly didn't mean to interrupt. I can let you go."

"No, please don't. I enjoy the nightly recap from you. It's different but fun."

"What do people normally do?" Leo asked, his tone curious.

"Post a little follow-up note on the site," Nick reminded him. "The one *you* set up, remember?"

"Ohh right. That one."

They both laughed.

"And not everyone has my private phone number," Nick pointed out.

"Oh." Leo went silent. "I—I shouldn't take advantage of—"

"Nah, you're fine," Nick assured him. "Seriously. I like the feedback."

"Ugh, I guess I should go get my jacket," Leo said with a sigh.

"You're still on the date?" Nick asked. "I thought you were on your way home or something!"

"Well, technically he was the one who walked away all huffy mid-date," Leo said. "So I doubt he'll rate me very highly either. But yeah, we were barely halfway through the wine tasting."

"How was the event otherwise?"

"It would have been fantastic with anyone else."

"I am sorry you missed out on an enjoyable evening," Nick said.

"It's okay. I've had a way better time talking to you than Andrew 'Twinkle Toes' Mulford so it wasn't a complete waste." Leo snorted.

Nick chuckled and ruefully thought, *I've had a better time talking to you than Alannah too*, though he didn't say it aloud.

He didn't want to give Leo the wrong impression.

He hesitated, wondering what he *should* say. "Well, we'll have to keep trying to find you someone."

"I guess so."

Nick hated the gloomy note in Leo's voice. "Hey," he said softly. "You're a *great* guy. A great catch. Matchmaking isn't guaranteed to be successful overnight, Leo. It's only been two dates and I had three new people sign up for the service yesterday. We have options!"

"Yeah, okay," Leo grumbled.

"Hey, if it makes you feel any better, I think my sister tried to set me up tonight. There's a very attractive woman who has been trying very hard to get my attention and I …" He tilted his head back, staring at the night sky. "I'm not feeling it."

"I guess it's never easy finding love," Leo said quietly.

It was for me, Nick thought wistfully. Being with Nicole had been as easy as breathing. But few people met the love of their life at eighteen and, apparently, even fewer got to enjoy their happily ever after for their whole life.

"We'll find love for you," Nick said earnestly. "I promise."

"Thanks, Nick. Enjoy your night." Leo's voice was very soft.

"Yeah, you too. Whatever you can salvage of it, anyway. And

I'll send you details about your next date tomorrow. I have someone in mind already."

"Thanks. G'night."

"Night, Leo."

Nick ended the call and slipped his phone in his pocket.

He went back into the house, shivering when the warm air hit him and he thawed a little. He hadn't realized how cold he'd gotten. Still, it had been worth it to do another post-date debrief with Leo.

The dinner had broken up and people were now talking in small clusters in the living room or helping clear the table.

Nick swiped a stack of plates, then carried them into the kitchen, knowing he'd likely find Heather there.

She was exactly where he'd expected, washing the more delicate dishes that wouldn't fit in the dishwasher.

"Sorry I bailed on you," he said, setting the dirty dishes to her left. He reached for a dish towel and went to work drying the large bowl on her right.

"No problem. Who was it on the phone?" Heather arched an eyebrow at him.

"Umm," Nick said, swiping the towel across the bowl intently. "Just Leo. We were, uh, talking website stuff."

Which was … sort of true.

"I thought it was all complete?"

"Oh, it is. But he's doing a test run. I offered him my matchmaking services for free in exchange for feedback on the process."

"Don't you have like a dozen testimonials from people raving about your services?"

"I do," Nick agreed, turning away to put the bowl on the shelf. "But it's good to get an outside perspective, no? Especially now that the process has changed a little. He's made some fantastic suggestions."

"Sure," Heather said slowly. "That makes sense."

"And I've never really had anyone to offer feedback in the same way," he explained. "I keep striking out on matching him up too. Poor Leo. He sounds bummed."

"Nick …" Heather said slowly. "Do think maybe—"

"Oh, there you are, Heather! And Nick. I wondered if you'd left completely."

He turned to see Alannah shooting him a bright grin. She was beautiful, interesting, and seemed like a very nice woman. He should feel something. Some flicker of interest.

Nope. Not a damn thing.

"Sorry." Heather dried her hands. "Are you heading out already, Lana?"

Alannah had her purse draped over her shoulder. "I am. Sorry. Busy day tomorrow."

"No worries. Glad you could come."

"Let me go get your coat. I'll be right back."

"Thanks."

Once they were alone in the kitchen, Alannah stepped forward. "I had a nice time meeting you tonight, Nick."

"I enjoyed meeting you too," he said sincerely.

She wet her lips, tucking her hair behind her ear. "Would you be interested in a date sometime?"

"I'm sorry, no," he said, hating the way her hopeful expression fell. "I enjoyed talking to you. I just don't think I'm there yet. You understand?"

She nodded, her expression turning rueful. "It's all about the timing."

"It is."

"Well," she said lightly. "Maybe I'll have to sign up for your matchmaking service then."

He smiled. "Well, no high-pressure sales tactics here, I promise, but I'd be happy to help you meet someone if you're interested."

"Thanks." She held out a hand which he shook. "And thanks for letting me down nicely."

Once Heather returned with Alannah's coat and walked her to the door, Nick resumed drying dishes, feeling a touch guilty, but mostly relieved.

Later, after the rest of the guests had cleared out and it was only Nick sitting in his sister's living room drinking a glass of wine with her and her wife, he said. "I think you were starting to ask me something earlier, Heather. What was it?"

She shrugged. "Nothing important. Hope you didn't mind me inviting Alannah."

"Were you trying to set us up?" he asked, curious.

She waggled her hand. "Sort of? Just thought you were both nice, attractive single people. Figured you might hit it off. I didn't want to be pushy though."

“I appreciate that,” he said. “I—I’m focused on looking for love for other people right now though. You get that, right?”

“I do,” Heather said slowly. “I just hope you don’t spend too long worrying about everyone but yourself.”

CHAPTER SEVEN

Leo was the first to arrive at the Parade of Lights for date number three.

He glanced around, but although there were crowds of people already assembling, bachelor number three was nowhere in sight. His name was Dylan and they'd texted a little bit before the event. Nick had suggested Leo try that, since the first two dates had gone pretty terribly.

Online, Dylan had seemed like a super nice, ordinary guy. He worked as a large animal vet tech and helped take care of the reindeer in town. It was such a cool job. Dylan had a great smile in the photos Leo had seen, and had a good sense of humor.

Leo was hopeful.

Maybe Dylan was running late. *Tons* of people came from out of town to the event and parking was scarce. Leo was lucky he could walk from his apartment to the park where they'd agreed to meet.

With a shrug, Leo glanced around Sugar Plum Park.

Several food trucks were set up and he made a beeline for the one from Ginger's Bread. It was new—a big project Joel had been working on in the past year—and decorated with a cute little gingerbread person.

While Leo waited in line, he kept an eye out for Dylan and checked his phone a number of times. But neither the guy, nor a message, appeared.

It was nearly twenty minutes after their agreed-on meeting time when Leo finally reached the front of the line and Dylan was nowhere to be found.

"I'm going to need your largest cookie and some mulled cider," Leo said with a heavy sigh. "And booze if you've got it."

Joel's laugh quickly turned into a worried expression. "Hey, you okay?"

"No," Leo said morosely. "I think I've been ghosted."

"Oh no! You had high hopes for him too."

"We'll see," Leo said, frowning. "But yeah. So far? Bleh."

"How about some holiday spice churros dunked in chocolate orange sauce and a tall mulled cider?" Joel offered. "I'm afraid we don't have a liquor license but I'm sure there's a nice Christmas Falls resident carrying a flask of something who you could hook up with."

"Hell yes to the churros and mulled cider. And I was kidding about the booze. Mostly."

Joel grinned.

After Leo paid and he had a hot steaming paper cup of cider in one hand and a container of churros with dipping sauce in hand, Joel said, "I hope your date shows up!" with a cheerful wave.

"Me too," Leo said ruefully. But he thanked Joel and stepped away from the truck so the next person could get their order.

He was debating how to juggle both items and actually get them in his face when Nick appeared. "Do you need some help with that?"

"Uhh, yes please," Leo said gratefully as he handed his cup of cider over. "Thank you."

Nick took it, frowning at him. "So, what happened to your date? I thought you were meeting up here tonight."

"Well, we were supposed to." Leo checked his phone again. "But I don't know where Dylan is and I've heard nothing from him."

"Have you tried texting him?"

"Not yet. I didn't want to be impatient if he had trouble parking or something. But we've officially passed that point." Leo typed out a message. ***Hey. Wanted to check to see if you're okay. I'm at the meeting spot and I don't see you anywhere. We did say 5:15 at Sugar Plum Park, right?***

When Leo was done, he stuffed his phone in his coat pocket and glanced up to see Nick looking at him with a worried frown.

"What?" he asked, feeling self-conscious.

"I feel terrible this is going so badly for you," Nick said, sounding frustrated.

Leo shrugged and picked up a churro. He dunked the fried dough in the chocolate sauce and took a bite, moaning a little at the taste while he prayed he hadn't singed off every last taste bud.

Holy fuck that was good. But steaming hot.

"Story of my life," Leo said with a sigh as he fanned his mouth. "It's fine. Either I'll hear from him or I won't."

"I appreciate your ability to bounce back from disappointment so well," Nick said. "But I'm sorry to be the *cause* of your disappointment."

"Hey, it's not you," Leo assured him. "Seriously, it was like this in Chicago too. I have bad luck dating or something, I swear. I'm like, cursed or something."

"Yeah, but—"

"Churro?" he asked, thrusting the little cardboard container out because he couldn't stand the sight of Nick looking so glum on his account. "They're holiday spice flavored and the dipping sauce is chocolate orange. They're delicious."

He didn't want to hear Nick apologize again. It wasn't his fault Leo was a magnet for bad dates. Okay, maybe the last few were his fault but this really was par for the course for Leo.

"Sure." Nick slipped off his glove and took one.

The look of bliss crossing his face when he ate it was like a sudden gut punch to Leo's system.

Oh man, what Leo wouldn't give to have been the one to cause Nick to look like that. In bed, rather than from some food his friend had made.

"*Wow* those are good," Nick said.

"Joel knows his stuff," Leo agreed. "I am going to gain like forty pounds living above the bakery and I do not care. I swear, everything they make there is good for the soul."

Nick smiled. "You'll look fantastic either way. And I agree. I've never had anything bad there."

"Well, feel free to share these," Leo said, waggling the container of churros and trying to ignore his sudden flush at the compliment. "I had a hearty dinner so I'm getting full already."

"Yeah?"

"Yeah, I made my mom's baked spaghetti and meatballs recipe and it was freaking fantastic. I hadn't made it in a while and it hit just right, you know?"

"Ooh, you'll have to share the recipe with me," Nick said, helping himself to another churro. "It sounds delicious."

"Thanks. I will."

Leo reached for the cup of cider, taking it from Nick's hand. "Hmm. I wonder if this has cooled down enough to drink."

Nick took the container of churros and Leo pried the lid off the cider. "Nope, still fucking hot." He put the lid back on, glanced around, then checked his phone again.

"Any news?" Nick asked.

"Nope."

Nick frowned. "Leo, I am so—"

"Shush." Leo quieted him with a wave of his hand. "None of that! Dylan is innocent until proven guilty. For all I know, something terrible happened. For his sake, I hope not. For mine … well, it would soothe my ego a little."

He laughed, shrugging. "But seriously. I *refuse* to dwell on it. He stood me up and I won't know until later if it was intentional or not so I'm not going to think about it right now. I want to enjoy the parade and my yummy snacks and make the best of a disappointing evening, okay?"

It was either that or break down crying in the middle of Sugar Plum Park and fuck that.

Nick gave him a soft smile. "You're a good person, Leo. I'm glad you don't let anyone's poor behavior dim that."

"Someday, my prince will come," Leo said with a little sigh. "But tonight is not that night. I'm sure you have other plans though, so don't let me keep you from that. It looks like people are assembling to go watch the parade."

He nodded to the people streaming out of the park toward the sidewalk where the parade would pass by.

"Well." Nick rubbed the back of his neck and Leo noticed he didn't wear a wedding ring. "About that. I kinda came here tonight for you."

"Yeah?" Leo tilted his head. "What do you mean?"

"I wasn't going to say hi or anything. I just wanted to be around if your date got creepy. You totally handled the previous guys fine but I—I felt a little responsible and wanted to be here if you needed any help."

"That's so sweet," Leo said, his heart melting.

"So, um, what do you say we enjoy the parade together? I know I'm only the consolation prize but … might be fun?"

Oh, buddy, Leo thought wistfully. *You are so far from being a consolation prize it's ridiculous. You would be the ultimate grand prize to anyone who got to keep you. Nicole was a lucky, lucky woman.*

"That would be fun," Leo said aloud. "If you don't mind."

"Mind? Nah, I always enjoy talking to you." Nick's smile was warm and a little flutter appeared in the center of Leo's chest.

Oooh this was *such* a bad idea but there was no way in hell he'd turn down a chance to spend the evening with Mr. Tall, Dark, and Handsome.

Munching on the churros, Leo and Nick crossed the park, following the crowds toward the street and Leo's excitement grew as they worked their way toward a spot where they might be able to see the parade go by.

Nick got stopped by a couple who thanked him warmly for setting them up, and one of the guys proudly showed off the daughter they'd adopted recently.

"That's my favorite part of being a matchmaker," Nick said, beaming at him as the family walked away. "Seeing how happy people are and knowing I got to take part in it."

"I love that," Leo said softly.

Nick was so good at his job. It wasn't his fault Leo had the worst luck ever when it came to dates.

They found a spot along the parade route and Leo glanced around. People were dressed in warm layers of clothing and some had light-up headbands and glowsticks around their necks. In the distance, Leo could hear the sound of the marching band tuning up.

"So how was your Thanksgiving?" Leo asked, turning back to face Nick. "Do anything fun?"

"Yeah, I had dinner with my family. My parents live in town."

"Oh nice," Leo said. "I didn't know that."

"Yeah, it's great. I get to see them frequently. What about you?"

"Oh! I had dinner at Joel and Hayden's new place. That was fun too. We had it kinda early in the day so I came home after, then sacked out and watched hockey."

"You're a hockey fan?" Nick asked, sounding surprised.

"I am. I know I don't look it."

"Oh, I didn't mean it like that. You just didn't put it on your list of hobbies."

"Oops, must have forgotten. It's kinda new, honestly. I started watching last season. Joel is related to Jamie Walsh. He plays for the—"

"Evanston River Otters," Nick finished, tossing the empty churro container in the trash.

"Yeah." Leo brightened. "You're a fan too?"

"Oh definitely. I mean, Heather—my sister—and her wife are super into women's hockey and we go to games sometimes. I kinda got invested in the Otters a few years ago too though, when the players started coming out."

"It's funny, I was never into it all but Hayden kept raving about how awesome the team was and that they were totally queer. Last spring, Hayden and Joel came to Chicago to visit and we all went to see an Otters game. They lost, because they're like *terrible* right now, but we had a blast. I had no idea I'd ever be into sports but add some queer players and I am so on board," Leo said grinning.

He'd gone a little overboard, talking fast and practically bouncing around as he spoke. He grimaced. Lots of people told him they found it annoying. But Nick merely smiled.

"Yeah, that's great. I am envious you got to see them play live though. That sounds fun."

"We had a *blast.*" Leo took a sip, enjoying the warmth of the spiced cider. "And we got to go back to meet some of the players. Jamie Walsh is so nice and his husband is super cute. I mean, like all of the players were ridiculously hot. But, sadly, all taken, as far as I could tell. At least the gay ones."

He let out a self-conscious little laugh. "Oh, but you probably don't want to hear about me drooling over dudes."

Nick shot him a quizzical look. "Why? It's not like I mind—"

A loud cheer broke out from the crowd and Leo glanced up to see a festive banner held by two warmly dressed people round the corner, a brightly lit firetruck behind them.

"Ooh," Leo said, excited. "It looks like the parade is starting!"

Leo was *adorable.*

His enthusiasm and energy were infectious and Nick spent as much time watching Leo take in the parade as he did watching it himself.

Despite the crappy way Leo's evening had started, he threw himself into the festivities with his whole being. He cheered loudly at the firetruck with Santa's sleigh and reindeer atop it and caught candy thrown to the crowd, handing it off to nearby kids who weren't tall enough to grab it on their own.

He chatted excitedly to the people next to him, beaming when they offered him a splash of spiced rum for his cider.

From the floats designed to look like a train to the marching band from the local community college playing *Here Comes Santa Claus*, the entire event was a celebration of holiday cheer. It was cheesy and silly and so much more fun with Leo excitedly grabbing his arm to point out something he'd spotted.

Nick enjoyed the event for the first time in years.

When it was over, and the crowd dispersed, Leo turned to him, his face glowing as much as the floats had been.

"That was amazing," he said, bouncing on his toes. "I *loved* that!"

"I'm so glad," Nick said honestly. Because what could have been an awful evening for Leo had wound up being fun for both of them and he appreciated how full of life Leo was. How joyous and optimistic he seemed. "Thanks for letting me tag along with you."

"Yeah, any time!" Leo stuffed his hands in his pockets. His cheeks were pink-tinged and he looked so cozy in his parka and knitted winter hat, scarf, and gloves. "Well, I guess I should say goodnight. I'm uh, heading back to my place."

"Oh, I'm, uh, walking that direction anyway," Nick said, oddly reluctant to see the night end. "If you want to stick with me. Wouldn't want you to get lost."

Leo shot him an amused glance but nodded. "Sure. Sounds good."

"So how are you settling into Christmas Falls?" Nick asked as they followed the wave of people dispersing, heading back to their homes for the evening or to enjoy the rest of the evening at a bar or restaurant.

Leo smiled. "Honestly, it's been great. Everyone is so friendly. Cassie—who works at the bakery—I met her husband at Thanksgiving and he seems great. We're going to grab a drink sometime. As friends," he added hastily.

Nick smiled. "I didn't think you were planning on dating him. As far as I know, they're monogamous. And you indicated you were too on the form ..."

"Yeah, I am," Leo said. "I mean, no shade to people who aren't. I ... I guess I'm not wired that way. I want to make a life with someone. One person. Like, I don't want to make them my *whole* world. I think it's important people have outside interests and other friends and stuff but you know, I want to come home to my *person*, you know?"

"I get that," Nick said softly. "I had that."

"I can't imagine how hard it is when you lose them," Leo said, his voice filled with so much compassion it made Nick's chest ache.

"It's like a part of me went missing," he whispered.

"Do you think you'll ever look for it again?" Leo asked.

"I do," Nick said firmly. "I don't know when. But Nic would *haunt* me if I gave up on love for myself permanently."

"Well, be careful," Leo said, his voice gently teasing. "It is Christmas. You might find yourself haunted by three ghosts."

Nick chuckled. "True. Though I'm not much of a Scrooge."

"No. You seem like a very nice person."

Nick glanced over at him. Being called a nice person was often an insult or at least, a mediocre compliment. But the sincerity and warmth in Leo's eyes dispelled any thoughts it was either. "Thank you."

They slowed to a stop and Nick realized he'd walked Leo all the way to his door instead of splitting off and turning onto Prancer Street.

"I hope I end up with someone half as good as you someday," Leo said earnestly.

"I promise I'll do better next time with your date," Nick said, desperately wanting Leo to believe him. "There's a guy named Jett who I want you to meet. I haven't had much luck finding him a date—and I *swear* it has nothing to do with him—he's great. I think you'll hit it off."

"Yeah?" Leo asked dubiously.

"He's a coder, so I'm sure you have a fair amount in common with work."

"True."

"And he's good-looking and seems very normal!"

"Yeah?"

Nick smiled. He could hardly blame Leo for being a little skeptical of that. "I mean, I can't promise he won't randomly show up dressed like Mrs. Claus or something—"

Leo chuckled.

"But he's gotten great feedback from other people. He hasn't found the right person yet but I have a good feeling you two will hit it off," Nick said firmly.

"I hope so," Leo said. "Because so far, *this* is the best date I've ever been on."

He must have seen the look on Nick's face because he let out an awkward laugh and hastily added, "not that this was a date or anything. I mean, you're straight and not looking for love right now and—"

Nick winced. "I'm not—I'm not straight, Leo."

Leo's jaw dropped and he blinked at Nick. "You're not?"

"No. I'm bi," he said. "You're right about the fact that I'm not looking for love right now, but when I am, I'm open to falling in love with anyone."

"Oh. Sorry. I shouldn't have assumed …"

Nick's smile was rueful. People always did. Even ones in the LGBTQ+ community. Because he'd been married to a woman, they'd assumed he was straight. He shrugged. "It happens."

"Yes, but I should know better. I'll *do* better."

The sincerity in Leo's voice and gaze made Nick believe it. "Thanks," he said softly. "And I hope you didn't take what I said the wrong way. It's not … it's not that I *wouldn't* date you, Leo. You're a fantastic guy, handsome, incredibly interesting to talk to. I'm not …"

"It's not me, it's you?" Leo said and there was a wry little twist to his lips.

Nick chuckled. "Pretty much."

"Hey, I get it." Leo reached out and squeezed his upper arm. "No hard feelings. You aren't ready to date and I understand why."

"Thanks. I did enjoy spending the evening with you," Nick admitted. "Honestly. I'd like it if we were friends."

Leo nodded, licking his lips. They were fuller than Nick had realized. Softer looking. "I'd like that too. G'night, Nick."

"Night, Leo." As Nick turned and walked away, a little dazed.

A small piece of him felt guilty for being grateful Dylan hadn't shown up tonight. If he had, Nick would have missed out on a fantastic evening with Leo and he wasn't sure what to make of that.

He'd said he'd wanted to be friends with Leo, and that was true. But was it the *whole* truth?

CHAPTER EIGHT

"So whatever happened with the guy who stood you up?" Hayden asked Leo the following night as they sat at a booth at The Snowflake Shack.

Leo was thoroughly enjoying his mushroom Swiss burger and he held up a finger to tell Hayden his mouth was full.

"Dylan?" Leo asked a moment later, shrugging. "Nothing much. He texted me this morning and was super apologetic, but ..."

"What was his excuse?" Hayden asked around a mouthful of his bacon cheeseburger.

"Food allergy."

"Think it was legit?"

"Yeah." Leo sighed. "So, like, apparently, he was eating at Rudy's before the parade and had a very unexpected shellfish allergy. I heard people talking about it this morning at the bakery."

"Ooh, yeah, I did too. I didn't realize it was *your* guy though."

"Not my guy," Leo said with a wry smile. "Apparently the waiter rushed in with an epi pen and saved Dylan's life, then after his shift, went to the ER to check up on him. And now they're going on a date. I mean, what the fuck, Hayden? How does literally *everyone* in this fucking town get their goddamn meet-cute and happily ever after like they're living in some freaking Hallmark cozy holiday rom-com when I'm fucking living in some depressing indie piece about the futility of hope."

Hayden snickered. "Yikes. Sorry I asked."

"No, it's fine." Leo waved his hand. "I'm happy for Dylan. Honestly. It's just … it fucking *sucks* to always be on this side of things."

"Hey, I get that," Hayden said softly. "But you gotta be patient."

"I *am* being patient," he grumbled. "Can't you tell?"

"Ohh yeah, definitely. So patient." Hayden rolled his eyes. "So what next?"

He shrugged. "I dunno. This morning, Nick sent me some info for a couple more guys he's matched me with. I've got two dates this weekend, then one next week with some dude named Jett, who Nick seemed convinced will be a good match. I dunno."

"What about the first two?"

Leo shrugged. "Honestly, we've texted a little but I don't even remember their names. They seem fine. Perfectly nice guys who appear to be varying degrees of kind and funny and handsome."

"Well, that doesn't exactly sound bad." Hayden crunched into an onion ring.

"I know."

They liked the holidays but not too much. They were looking for the same things Leo was and were able to hold a decent conversation via text. They just didn't seem like they had the potential for the romantic sparks Leo longed for.

Not the way there had been the night of the parade with Nick, anyway.

Leo would swear, for a moment, as they said goodnight outside of Leo's door, Nick had been staring at his mouth. That he'd looked at Leo as more than a client or a friend. And gah, a part of him wished he didn't know Nick was bi.

Which made Leo feel guilty because just because Nick was bi didn't mean he was available or ready to date. He'd made that fucking clear. And Leo wanted to be respectful of that.

But *damn*. He and Nick had a good connection. If Nick wasn't available, why did it feel like he was the only person Leo had been able to find that with?

He said as much to Hayden, who winced. "I think you're being a little unrealistic. You expect the magic to happen *immediately* and you're totally writing these guys off before you give them a chance. Sometimes feelings take a while to develop."

Leo winced too. "True."

"I get that you want this magical romance to happen but I feel like you want it so bad you're putting *a ton* of pressure on yourself and your dates and not letting it happen *organically*. It'll happen when it's meant to."

"When did you of all people get all philosophical and romantic?" Leo asked with a snort. He remembered Hayden as being pragmatic and a bit cynical.

Hayden shrugged. "Last Christmas, I guess? I dunno, blame Joel."

Despite his grouchiness, Leo chuckled, dragged a fry through a puddle of ketchup mixed with mustard.

"And I hate to say this, but you've been talking to Nick a lot lately, right?" Hayden said, leaning forward.

Leo winced. "Yeah. I usually call him after my dates for a debrief. And we've been texting some. About, like, a TV show we both watch and the Otters games and stuff though. Nothing big."

"Don't you think that's a bad idea?"

Leo made a face. "I mean, maybe?"

"It seems like you have a serious crush on him."

"Well, it's hard not to," Leo pointed out.

"Dude, I get that. I've seen him around town and talked to him a little. I get why you're into him. But he's *straight*."

"Uh, yeah, not so much," Leo admitted quietly. "He's bi. Just not ready to date."

"Oh. Huh," Hayden said thoughtfully. "Really?"

"Yeah. And, like, it was *bad* before," Leo said. "But when a guy is straight you go, 'damn, that's disappointing' but you wall them off in your head as not an option."

"Sure."

"But now there's no wall!" Leo slumped, resting his chin on his hand, fries forgotten. "So like, I'm supposed to forget the perfect fucking guy exists?"

"The perfect guy is also one who is actually available and interested in you," Hayden pointed out.

Leo glared. Damn him for being *logical and reasonable.*

"I know that," Leo protested. "But I … I don't know how to stop thinking Nick and I would be *so good* together."

Leo thought of the late-night conversations they'd had. The low, soft rumble of Nick's voice in Leo's ear and the way it made him feel.

Hayden leaned forward. "I'm worried about you. You're—you're hung up on someone who has made it clear they aren't ready to date. And I think spending so much time talking to him is making it harder for you to open up to the guys who *are* ready to date. You need to give the guys you have actual dates with a fair shot. There might not be a big spark at first but you might be good together if you give it a *chance*."

"I guess," Leo said with a sigh. "The problem is, they all seemed interchangeable. None of them stood out to me. Although I haven't talked to Jett yet. At least his *name* is memorable. And I think Nick said something about him being a coder, so we do have something in common there."

"Good! Yeah, that sounds promising. Just try not to compare these guys to Nick. Give them a chance to prove they're good for you without writing them off before you ever give them a chance."

"I …" Leo sighed. "Yeah, okay. You're right. I'll try."

"Good. I think you need to keep putting yourself out there," Hayden said encouragingly. "And when you do, you'll find the right guy, I know it."

"I fucking better," Leo muttered. "This is getting depressing."

Hayden snorted. "Damn. I thought I had the market cornered on bad moods around the holidays. Guess not."

"Yeah, but you had a good reason for it," Leo groused. "You were grieving your dad."

"I was," Hayden said. "But remember, Nick is grieving too."

"I know!" Leo sighed. "I know that. And I'm not mad at him for not being ready for a relationship. It … it sucks. But I can also recognize when I'm being ridiculous."

Hayden shrugged. "Hey, I get it. This is something you really want. And it's hard to keep getting rejected over and over. It was similar for me when I was looking for jobs."

"Yeah."

"It hurts to get your hopes up and have them knocked down."

"It does."

"So, think of Nick this way. He's perfectly qualified for the job. But he doesn't have any available openings right now."

Leo snickered.

Hayden threw a balled-up napkin at his head. "Shut up! You know what I mean."

"Yeah, well, I have plenty of available openings but no one wants to fill them," Leo grumbled.

Hayden, the asshole, had the nerve to laugh.

"Should I be worried?" Heather asked a few days later as she gave Nick a hug inside his front door. "You don't usually call me to come over to talk like this. Or, at least, not recently."

Nick sighed, squeezed his sister tight, then drew back. "Maybe a little worried?"

"Are you having a hard time with the holidays?" she asked, shrugging out of her coat, her brow furrowed with concern. "I know you struggled the past few years …"

"Oh, no," Nick said hastily. "No. I'm feeling good about the holidays this year. Come see the tree. I put it up a few days ago."

"Yeah?"

He let her kick off her boots and put them on the mat to drip-dry before he answered. "Yeah, go in the living room. I'll grab us tea, then meet you in there in a few."

When he carried a tray in, Heather stood by the Christmas tree. He'd added a few cookies from Ginger's Breads, because he hadn't been able to resist them when he stopped in the other day.

"The tree looks beautiful," Heather said, sounding surprised as she turned to face him. "You got some new decorations, huh?"

He nodded, setting the tray on the coffee table. “Yeah. I haven’t felt like decorating in a few years but I had the urge the other day, so I dragged the totes out of the attic. I got the lights on but when I opened the boxes of ornaments, it …” He hesitated, unsure of how to put it all into words. “It felt like I was trying to recreate something long gone.”

An expression of sympathy crossed her face. “I get that.”

“And it wasn’t even the ornaments Nic and I collected over the years that made me sad.” It was more wistfulness than anything. “I just, I don’t know. I needed a fresh start or something.”

He took a seat on the sofa.

“Well, that’s good right?” Heather asked, sitting near him. “You’re moving on in a healthy way.”

“It is good,” he agreed. “Nic wouldn’t want me wallowing and I don’t want to wallow either.”

“But that’s not why you wanted me to come over?”

“No.”

“Okay …”

“Sorry.” He took the teabag out of the pot, then filled the two mugs. The scent of gingerbread spice rose in the air. “I’m not trying to be mysterious about it. I ran into Ford the other day.”

“Ahh. Ford Donnelly, I presume?” She reached for a mug, cradling it.

“Yeah.”

Heather winced, shifting to rest her back against the arm of the sofa. “How is Nic’s brother doing?”

"I'm—I'm not sure. I went to Season's Readings to grab some new books and ran into him and Charlie there."

"Gosh, she must be getting big."

"She is," Nick said, feeling wistful. "I had hoped we'd stay close after Nic was gone but I really think we were both so buried in our grief we pushed each other away instead of leaning on each other like we should have."

"Hey, everyone deals with grief in different ways," Heather said softly.

"I know." Nick sighed. "I *do* know that. And I know Ford and I were both struggling back then. I just feel terrible for my part in what happened. But seeing Charlie—Ford's former stepdaughter—it really hit me. She doesn't live in Christmas Falls but I—I thought of her like a niece and I haven't seen her since Nic's death. Seeing how quickly time has passed made it hit home how long she's been gone. Charlie didn't even *know* me, Heather. I missed out on so many years with both of them."

"That's tough."

Nick took a sip of his tea, then winced because it was still too hot. "Yeah. I really regret the way my relationship with Ford fell apart after Nicole's death. I *miss* having more extended family."

Heather patted his knee. "I know you do. You've been an amazing uncle to Mimi and Sammi."

Nick smiled, though it fell after a moment as he thought more about his conversation with Ford. "I'm also worried because I think Ford is struggling."

"Emotionally or financially?"

"Possibly both, but I meant financially. Charlie wanted this stuffed animal I'm pretty sure he couldn't afford but when I offered to pay, he shot me down. Seemed offended I'd even asked." Nick's voice cracked and he stared down at his mug.

"That's rough."

"I …" Nick swallowed past the thickness in his throat. "When I lost Nicole, I didn't just lose my wife. I lost a guy I thought of as a brother, you know?"

"I know."

"And maybe I approached it the wrong way at the bookstore, but I wanted a chance to see him and Charlie again. I always thought of them as family and Nicole's death didn't *have* to change that."

Heather reached out, squeezing his forearm gently. "I'm sorry this has been so hard for you, Nick."

"Thanks." He sighed, then took a sip of his tea. "It's just painful to realize how differently things could have gone."

"I know. I wish I had some good advice for you."

"It's okay," Nick said with a little frown. "I just needed someone to vent to. Thanks for listening."

He'd been tempted to talk to Leo about it the other night when they did their usual debrief after his date but he'd hesitated.

Nick already struggled to keep Leo at a professional distance. He didn't need to make it any harder on himself.

"No dice."

Nick grimaced at the forlorn tone in Leo's voice as he got back from his latest date the same evening. "Damn. I hoped this one might be the one."

Leo laughed humorlessly. "Yeah, me too. No such luck. It wasn't terrible or anything. Just … no real connection."

Nick did the math. "That's what? Your fourth guy?"

"Yep. I should give up." He sighed, sounding defeated.

"So, usually it does happen pretty quickly, but the other day, one of my clients found their match on their *fifth* date," Nick said, trying to interject some cheerfulness into his voice. "What if that's you?"

Leo snorted. "*Sure.*"

"Hey, are you doubting my skills?" Nick teased.

"No, no, of course not," Leo said, giggling a little. "Sorry, I don't mean to be a jerk."

"You're not a jerk," Nick assured him, shifting onto his side and stroking Jelly's back. She was half-asleep, curled in a little ball next to him. He'd been reading before bed when Leo called. "You're just frustrated. Trust me, I get it."

He was frustrated too, but in a very different way.

It had been the oddest thing. He'd woken up in the middle of the night several times lately, hard and aching.

After Nicole's death, Nick's libido had taken an unsurprising nosedive. Once the initial intense grief had worn off, it had returned sporadically. He didn't actively think or dream about sex usually, and when he jerked off, it was more perfunctory than anything. A reflexive bodily need rather than a hot sweep of desire.

But lately ... it had come roaring back with a vengeance. And Nick would be lying if he said Leo hadn't starred in a few of those dreams.

One night a few days ago, he'd woken from a dream about kissing Leo. About threading his hand through his soft-looking hair and pressing their lips together. He'd dreamed of the sounds Leo would make and the way he'd wrap himself around Nick.

It was strange and startling and a little uncomfortable. Nick was glad he hadn't seen Leo in person lately because he was afraid he'd give himself away. Or *worse*, give Leo false hope.

"Hey, Nick?" Leo said now, his voice soft. "Did you fall asleep on me?"

"No, no." He cleared his throat. "Sorry. What were you saying?"

"Nothing, really. You got quiet on me."

"I guess I'm more tired than I realized."

"Yeah? Not sleeping well?" There was a sweet little thread of concern in Leo's voice that made Nick smile.

"Uhh." Nick wasn't sure how to answer that. "Weird dreams, I guess? I've been, um, waking up a lot, then having trouble getting back to sleep."

"You sound like Hayden. He's a chronic insomniac."

"Yeah? What does he do to deal with it?"

"Well, I think that's why he took up running. He does like 5 and 10k runs and half-marathons and shit."

"Hmm. Well, I have a regular workout routine. I'm not nuts about hitting the gym but I have a little workout area set up in the guest room. I try to get in some cardio and weights most days a week."

"Ugh, that's the one thing I miss about Chicago," Leo said wistfully. "I had a gym in my building. That was nice."

"What do you do now?"

"Walk a lot," he said. "And some bodyweight stuff. Anyway, yeah, maybe workouts won't solve your sleep issue. Do you know why you're waking up?"

"Mmm," Nick said, not sure how to answer that. He wasn't about to tell Leo he'd woken up thinking dirty thoughts about him. "Just a lot on my mind."

"Okay, so, I'm legitimately not trying to be a perv here, but do you know what usually helps me sleep?"

"No, what's that?" Nick asked warily.

"Well, getting myself off."

"Oh." Nick sucked in a sharp breath, his head suddenly filled with images of Leo stretched out in bed, touching himself.

"Shit! Sorry! I made it weird, didn't I?" Leo said with a groan in Nick's ear that did nothing to help the situation.

"Uhh." Nick rolled onto his back, trying to ignore the way his cock thickened. "No, I get what you're saying."

The cat jumped down with an annoyed noise, waving her tail in a disdainful swish as she walked through the open bedroom door for somewhere she wouldn't be disturbed.

"Like, it *does* work though," Leo said with a small laugh. "I'm honestly not trying to be weird here, I swear, I just thought if you hadn't tried it, you could?"

"I'll, um, take that under advisement," Nick said.

Leo snorted. "Shit, I *did* make you uncomfortable. God! I'm so sorry."

"No," Nick said, not wanting him to feel bad. "No. You just surprised me. I'll, uh, try it out. See if it helps."

"Yeah?" Leo's voice was soft now. Low.

"Yeah," Nick said, reaching down to adjust himself. His cock was trapped at an awkward angle in his underwear and he let out a little sigh of relief when everything was in a better position. "If I need to."

Like, the fucking *second* he got off the phone with Leo. Because while a part of Nick was tempted to touch himself now, he couldn't. He shouldn't. That would be crossing a line.

But he was absently rubbing himself through his clothes already. He pulled his hand away, biting back a groan.

"Well, um, I guess I'll let you go then?" Leo asked, his tone hesitant.

For one horrible moment, Nick wondered if he'd said the first part aloud but no, Leo was probably being polite.

"Yeah, I should, uh, try to get to bed early tonight. Might help me sleep too."

"Right. yeah, of course. Uhh, get some good sleep, Nick."

"You too," he said, wishing he could linger. "You too, Leo."

"Night," Leo said softly, then he was gone.

Nick ended the call, then took his earbuds out, dropping them onto the nightstand. He hesitated for a moment, then opened the drawer. There was a bottle of lube in there. He hadn't used it in ages, usually making do with conditioner in the shower.

But tonight …

Feeling guilty, Nick pulled it out. He shimmied his pajamas and underwear down to mid-thigh, then slicked his palm. He was hard and he hissed at the touch of cool gel on his sensitive skin.

But everything heated as he stroked, sliding his palm up and down the shaft. Fuck, that was good. It had been so long since he'd taken the time and allowed himself to enjoy masturbating. But desire rose hot and fast in his body tonight, flushing his skin and making his pulse throb in his groin.

Nick heard Leo's voice in his ear, urging him on, and he stroked, closing his eyes, guiltily imagining what Leo looked like under his clothes. He imagined the night after the parade when he'd walked Leo to his door, but rather than walking away with a friendly wave, he'd leaned in and whispered he wanted to kiss Leo.

He imagined Leo's gasp and the way he'd pull Nick closer.

It was so vivid it felt like a memory as it played out against his closed eyelids. The cool outside air and the warmth of Leo's mouth. The slick sweetness of his lips and tongue and the way he'd press close.

Nick could nearly taste the holiday spices on Leo's tongue and the soft sounds he'd let out as they pressed tightly together.

As he dragged his hand up and down his cock, he imagined

Leo fumbling to open the door and dragging him upstairs. "Want you," Leo would have whispered.

"Want you too," Nick would have said.

Because he did. Fuck, he *did* want Leo. He shouldn't, but he did.

And he trembled as the force of his desire hit him, imagining Leo tugging him into his bedroom and stripping them both off. Heated kisses and wandering hands and Leo's fresh winter scent in his nose as they rubbed off together. Slick and hot and …

With a rough shout, Nick came into his fist, pleasure boiling up and spilling out, flowing onto his skin.

Nick gasped in the quiet bedroom, body trembling, Leo's name on his lips as he shook through the orgasm.

"Oh my God," he whispered when he finally came back to himself, blinking up at the ceiling. "What the *fuck* was that?"

The best damn orgasm you've had in years, his brain replied helpfully.

With a groan, Nick reached for the tissues on the nightstand, mopping up the mess. When he was done, he let out a sigh, covering his eyes with his forearm. "What the hell do I do now?" he muttered.

But the only answer was Jelly hopping on the bed with a little *mrrrp*.

That was no help at all.

CHAPTER NINE

Leo walked to the back of The White Elephant and ducked into the room labeled The Nook, a special event space where trivia night was held. He glanced around hesitantly, half-afraid of what he'd find.

Along with the usual collection of townsfolk, one guy stood apart. He was ... damn, even hotter than he'd looked in the pics on his profile. He was around the same height as Leo, with dark hair, dark eyes, and tattoos covering both of his muscular biceps.

Best of all, he was dressed normally. No elf costumes this time. Although, admittedly, the last two dates Leo had been on weren't horrible. Just totally bland and forgettable.

The guy glanced over with a lopsided grin, then walked toward Leo. "Leo Fenner?"

"Yeah, hi. You're Jett Davis?"

"Yep."

"Oh thank God," Leo said before he could stop himself.

Jett gave him a quizzical look. "What were you expecting?"

"Um, one date I had was with a guy who showed up in an elf costume, so …"

Jett laughed. "Oh wow. Yeah that's, um, interesting."

"That was just the start of it," Leo said grimly. "But that's enough about him. You want to go grab a table? It looks like they're filling up fast. Do you have a team you're on?"

"No. Maybe we can join one?" Jett waved at the half-full tables.

Across the room, Stephanie waved and Leo brightened. "Oh, we should try over there. Stephanie was nice. I met her on a previous date."

Jett gave him a confused look. "I thought you were gay."

"Oh, I am." They wove through the tables to get to the far side of the room. "I sought refuge with her when the elf started to get creepy."

"Wow, and I thought I've been unlucky with my dates," Jett muttered.

"Seems to be going around."

They ordered drinks and made small talk with their new teammates. After the introduction was over, Jett turned to him.

"So, I heard you're new to town? How are you adapting to all the … cheer?"

Leo grinned. "Not gonna lie, it was a shock when I first visited. My friend Hayden warned me about it, but I never knew there could be this many Christmas puns."

Jett chuckled.

"But since the first visit, I quickly came to appreciate the town's quirkiness. It's one of the reasons I decided to move here and since I did, everyone made me feel real welcome," Leo said with a smile. He looked at his hands briefly, hiding his smile when he thought of Nick.

"Ooh, looks like we're about to start," Leo said when a woman walked up to the front of the room where a large whiteboard was set up. She introduced herself as Shelley and said she'd been MC-ing the trivia event.

She explained that no cell phones would be allowed so Leo tucked his into the pocket of his jacket hanging from the back of his chair and Jett put his away too.

"My servers will be keeping an eye on you, and if we see anyone looking for the answer online, your entire team will be automatically disqualified."

"There are four categories and ten questions per category," Shelley went on. "Tonight's categories are: Christmas carols, holiday traditions, Christmas entertainment, and the North Pole. We'll collect your forms at the end of each category and tally up the results for our leader board."

Leo glanced at Jett, frowning when he realized his attention was across the room, staring at the front door of the pub. Someone Leo didn't recognize walked in and Leo glanced away with a shrug and took a sip of his drink. Maybe Jett knew them or something.

Shelley continued. "We'll start it off easy with question one: how many reindeer fly and guide Santa Claus's sleigh?"

Stephanie laughed. "Well that's an easy one!"

Leo marked his answer on the trivia form, then glanced at Jett.

He'd been very quiet and he was staring at a nearby table. From this angle, Leo could see the guy Jett had been watching earlier, but the rest of the table was blocked from view by a tall guy wearing a Santa hat.

"Um, at the risk of making this super awkward, are you into the guy over there?" Leo whispered, nudging Jett with his elbow.

Jett choked. "Oh, God. I'm so sorry … I'm being terribly rude to you."

"No, it's okay," Leo said with a sigh. "I get it."

Jett shot him an understanding look. "Who are you pining over?"

"Uhh, I wouldn't say pining, exactly, but …" He smiled. "Well, his name is Nick."

Jett blinked. "The *matchmaker*?"

Leo nodded.

"Didn't he have a wife who passed away?" Jett asked, glancing back at the table.

"He did. He's totally not into me or anything," Leo said. "It's a stupid little crush on my part. I'll get over it."

"Not to freak you out or anything, but Nick's sitting over there with my guy."

Leo whipped his head around, blinking at the table. He had to crane his neck a little to see over the Santa hat guy, but once he did, he could see Nick's face in profile.

Leo glanced away just as fast, ducking down, not wanting Nick to see him. He'd already weirded Nick out with his talk of masturbation. *Gah.* Why hadn't he listened to Hayden?

But if Nick was weirded out, why the hell was he at The White Elephant when he knew this was where Leo would be tonight.

"What is he doing here?" Leo muttered to himself. Had Nick come to check on him? He'd done that at the parade …

But Leo shook his head, realizing it was stupid, pointless speculation. He glanced back at Jett who was staring at him with a curious expression.

"Anyway, your guy, huh?" Leo raised an eyebrow at Jett, who fidgeted, looking a little uncomfortable. Leo chuckled, then added, "Tell me about him."

Jett glanced over at the table again.

"I feel like I've been in love with Remy for half my life, but we only recently became friends. I was kind of an idiot in high school."

"Who wasn't?" Leo joked.

Jett smiled. "We're friends now. Which is great, I guess. But there are these moments, you know? Like he says something that gets my hopes all up, then firmly shoves me back into the friend zone. Sometimes I wish there was a sign out there to tell me if I even have a chance with him."

"Do you want to find out?" Leo asked as an idea popped into his head.

"Oh? What do you have in mind?"

Before Leo could answer, Shelley called for everyone to write down their final answers before they collected the forms. He grimaced, scribbled down a couple of answers that were probably wrong because he'd only been half-paying attention to the last few questions.

He stood, grabbing Jett's hand and pulling him to his feet. "Come with me."

Leo wove through the tables, right past where Nick and Remy and their friends were sitting. Leo didn't glance Nick's way, didn't stop until they were in the back near the bathrooms.

Leo spun Jett around until his back was against the wall, boxing him in with his arms.

Jett blinked, clearly startled. "What are you—"

"Are they watching?" Leo asked.

Jett peeked over his shoulder.

"We definitely have an audience," he muttered. "Is this all part of your grand plan?"

Leo grinned instead of replying and took a step closer till their chests were nearly touching. He reached up and brushed a loose piece of hair off Jett's forehead, looking deeply into his eyes.

Jett blinked at him, his gaze darting toward the table, so Leo cupped his cheek. "Don't look. Keep your eyes on me."

Jett wet his lips. "You're not going to kiss me, are you? Because while you're hot and all, I'm not interested in kissing someone in front of my crush."

Yeah, Jett was fucking hot too. But unlike every time Leo got close to Nick, there wasn't a single spark.

Damn it.

"What a coincidence, because same. We're not going to kiss, but maybe try and look like you *want* to kiss me," Leo teased.

Jett looked him in the eye, like he was studying Leo's face, before his gaze darted away again.

Leo was about to apologize and pull back because clearly Jett wasn't into Leo's plan when someone brushed his hand away from Jett's cheek, roughly saying, "We need to talk."

CHAPTER TEN

"What the fuck?" Nick muttered under his breath as he watched Remy pull Jett away from Leo's embrace.

But when Leo smirked, looking pleased with himself, Nick began to doubt Leo and Jett had hit it off the way Nick had originally thought.

The thought of Leo having a successful date should have made Nick *happy* but watching Leo pin Jett against a wall had sent an uncomfortably sharp jolt of irritation through him.

He'd hated the sight. He'd been *relieved* to see Remy break up the near kiss.

As Remy and Jett disappeared and Nick tried to figure out what in the hell had happened, Leo sauntered up, smiling, clearly not at all annoyed his date had disappeared with another man.

"Hey. What are you doing here?" Leo asked, his eyes twinkling.

"Uh, hey," Nick managed. "A couple of friends dragged me along. I wasn't spying on you, I promise."

Leo's grin slipped away, his expression turning assessing. "No?"

"No," Nick said firmly. He hadn't gone along with it because some part of him wanted to be closer to Leo. Because he wanted to be there in case the date went badly and …

Fuck, he definitely had.

"Right." Leo looked him up and down. "So, having a good time?"

"Uhh. Yeah, trivia's fun." Nick cleared his throat. "What about you? I'd ask how your date with Jett was going but he left with another man, so …"

Leo snorted. "Yeah, you missed the mark there, Mr. Matchmaker. Jett's totally into Remy. And, apparently, vice versa."

Nick winced. Jett had appeared reluctant to date lately, but how in the hell had he missed the mark so badly there? He was friends with Remy, for fuck's sake. He should have noticed something between them. Everything had been off since Leo arrived. Not that he blamed Leo. He was the one who was distracted.

"I am starting to think I'm atrocious at my job," Nick admitted with a sigh.

Leo's face softened. "Nah, you're not atrocious. Literally *everyone* in town raves about you."

"Except you and Jett."

"No, I think Jett is *very* happy with the way tonight's date went," Leo said with a laugh. "He got a shot at Remy."

Nick narrowed his eyes. "You did that on purpose."

"Fuck yeah I did," Leo said with a grin. "Look, no one likes a guy who gets creepy possessive. But a little bit of jealousy can be good. Pretending to make a move on Jett was an easy way to test if Remy had more than friendly feelings for him."

"And you don't care that you and Jett never got a shot at anything?"

"Nah." Leo shrugged. "He's hot and all and I'm sure we'll wind up friends but he's not my guy."

"Well, I'm glad you're not upset by it," Nick said slowly. "Hopefully the next date will go better though."

Leo looked away. "Yeah, I don't know, Nick. I'm starting to think I should take a break. Tonight didn't bother me but—"

"Excuse me," one of the servers said. "Are you using this table? Your friend paid a bit ago but we have other people waiting."

Nick glanced over to see that not only Remy was gone, but Kaysen had left too, probably called it a night too after both Remy and Nick had abandoned him and left him with the bill.

"Shit. Sorry," Nick said. He reached for his coat, snagging it off the chair where he'd draped it earlier. "I'm done here."

He glanced at Leo who had disappeared, weaving through the crowded tables to the table he'd been sitting at earlier. Leo spoke to the women sitting there, saying something to them that made them laugh and stand to give him a hug.

Nick smiled faintly. He liked how friendly Leo was. How easily he seemed to fit in this weird little town.

Leo appeared a few moments later, looking surprised. "Oh, you waited."

"We *were* in the middle of a conversation," Nick pointed out. "Maybe we can continue it on the way home? I can walk that way with you."

Although that would take about three minutes, since Ginger's Breads and The White Elephant were right next door. If they went out the back, they'd literally be *at* Leo's door. Still, Nick didn't mind the short walk.

Leo looked at him for a long moment before he nodded. "Sure. Sounds good."

It wasn't until they were on the sidewalk in front of the restaurant that either of them spoke.

"So you were saying you want a break from dating?" Nick asked as they turned right onto Prancer Street.

Leo zipped up his jacket, then stuffed his hands in his pockets. The air was cold and every breath made big gusts of steam flow from Leo's mouth.

"Yeah," he said softly. "I'm—I'm starting to feel like I'm in a weird place about it."

"What do you mean?" Nick asked.

"Like I'm trying too hard or something. I don't know. Hayden and I talked about it last week and I've had two totally boring dates since and I … I can't seem to get my head in the right spot about it."

"Okay …" Nick said slowly because he wasn't sure he understood what was wrong.

"It's starting to make me feel like there's something about *me* that is horribly unlikeable."

"Leo," Nick said, his heart aching as he finally understood what Leo was getting at. Because yeah, he knew Leo was bummed it wasn't working out but he hadn't realized he was starting to doubt himself.

"Well, I'm the common denominator," Leo said, his tone a little bitter. "Literally every fucking guy around me is pairing off, finding the love of their life. And I'm not. And, you know, I try to have a healthy ego. I know I have a lot to offer someone. So why does no one see it? Clearly, I'm doing something wrong."

"You're not doing anything wrong," Nick protested. They turned right onto Candy Cane Lane and he glanced over at Leo, his face silhouetted against the glow of the window on the side of The White Elephant.

"No? Then why doesn't anyone ever want to be with me?" Leo whispered.

I want you, Nick thought, but he bit his tongue and tried to think of another reason. A better reason. Something that wouldn't make Leo feel *worse*.

"I think so much of relationships comes down to timing and being in the right place at the right time," Nick said slowly. "And when it doesn't go well, it's about the wrong timing."

They reached the parking lot behind the restaurant and turned to face each other.

"It just *sucks*," Leo said, his eyes wide and filled with hurt. "What am I doing wrong? What is so wrong with me that no one—no one wants me?"

"Leo," Nick said, his heart aching. "It's not that no one wants you. Of course you're wanted."

"Yeah? And who is this mysterious guy who wants me so fucking badly?" Leo asked, his voice rising.

"I do," Nick whispered.

"Don't." Leo closed his eyes. "Don't mess with me, Nick. I can't take it. Not right now."

"I *wouldn't*," he protested. "I do want you. I …"

"Yeah." Leo glanced away. "Or you're trying to be *nice*."

He spat the last part like it was a dirty word this time.

"I'm not being *nice*, Leo" Nick argued. "God. If you only knew what I thought about after you hung up after every phone call lately."

Leo looked him in the eye again, lips parted. "Really?" he whispered.

"Really," Nick said roughly.

"Fuck." Leo shivered. "God. Me too."

Nick blinked. "You … you've been thinking about me too?"

Leo laughed softly. "I haven't thought about anyone else since we met."

Against his better judgment, Nick stepped forward. "Tell me what you think about, Leo," he said roughly. "Tell me what you imagine."

"I … I think about you kissing me. About your hands on my body. I picture how you look without your clothes on and how you'd feel if we were—"

Unable to stay away a second longer, Nick leaned in and covered Leo's mouth with his own. Leo moaned softly and the sound went straight to Nick's head.

Nick wrapped his arms around Leo, pulling him closer. He immediately responded, clutching Nick's coat and pressing his tongue between Nick's lips. Nick barely had a moment to register how Leo felt in his arms before he was swept away in the kiss, heat blazing through him like a match to dry tinder.

He backed Leo against the rough wall of the restaurant, kissing him desperately, drinking in every frantic gasp falling from Leo's mouth and the urgency in his touch.

When they were both breathless, panting, Nick drew back. His heart thudded against his breastbone as he stared at Leo's swollen lips and the half-lidded contentment of his eyes.

Leo reached up, tracing his thumb across Nick's lower lip, and Nick kissed it.

"My place or yours?" Leo rasped.

Nick frowned.

"Don't tell me you don't want me, Nick," Leo whispered, settling a hand on his chest. "If you aren't ready, that's fine. But don't tell me you don't want it."

"I do, but uh." Nick licked his suddenly dry lips, anxiety making his heart beat faster. "I've never been with a guy."

Leo shrugged like it was unimportant. "Do you want to be?"

"I want *you*," Nick admitted.

"Then I'll show you what I like," Leo said and he made it

seem so simple. So uncomplicated. "And I vote my place since it's like … twenty feet from here."

Nick swallowed and nodded, letting Leo take his hand and tow him across the parking lot and toward the bakery. Nick felt dazed as he followed Leo up the stairs and into his apartment, wondering if this was a dream.

But the apartment seemed very real. It was small and cozy looking. Warm.

Boots off, Nick's hands shook a little as he handed over his coat, watching Leo strip out of his outerwear too.

Leo certainly wasn't shy as he took Nick's hand again, pulling him into the bedroom. It was small too, the bed taking up most of the space, but Nick couldn't tear his gaze from Leo as he stripped off his sweater and T-shirt. Nick breathed shallowly as Leo stepped forward and removed his shirt too, carefully undoing each button, before he flung it away and pressed their bodies together.

Nick gasped at the feel of warm skin against his own, closing his eyes and blindly seeking Leo's mouth. It was almost too much. Too intense. It had been so long since he'd touched someone this way. So long since he'd kissed someone other than the woman he'd loved and lost.

He splayed his hands across Leo's back and pulled him closer. There was just heat and need as he pressed Leo down onto the bed. He got a handful of Leo's ass in his hand and squeezed, loving the way Leo moaned at the touch and bucked against him.

"Nick …"

The sound of his name on Leo's lips made him groan and bury his face against Leo's neck. He smelled good, like the pine-y winter cologne he wore and something else warm and unique to Leo.

"What do you want?" Leo asked softly, rolling them onto their sides. He skimmed a hand down Nick's body, cupping his dick where it pushed at the fly of his jeans.

"I don't know," Nick admitted, overwhelmed by the touch. After such a long drought, it verged on the edge of too much.

"I could suck your dick," Leo said, pressing a kiss to his jaw. "Or you could fuck me."

"I … both sound incredible," Nick admitted, finally looking him in the eye.

"I'm guessing you haven't had sex in a while," Leo asked with a little smile. "Anything I should be worried about?"

It took Nick a minute to work out what he meant but when he did, he shook his head. "No. Nothing." He'd only ever had sex with one person.

"Good. Me either. I got tested before I moved here." Leo grinned and shimmied down the bed.

Nick stared at Leo, lips parted, as he undid Nick's belt, button, and zipper. He lifted his hips when Leo coaxed him to and moments later, he was bare except for his underwear.

Leo reached down, rubbing his cock through the fabric. Nick let out a low groan, biting his lip.

"Leo …" He felt wound tight, too sensitive, head whirling at the onslaught of sensations.

Leo's grin widened. "I've got you."

He tugged the boxer briefs down and Nick's cock slapped against his stomach, hard and aching already.

"Oh, look at you," Leo said breathily. "*Fuck*."

"Yeah?" Nick asked, voice strained because Leo had taken him in hand, his palm warm as he smoothed it up and down Nick's shaft.

"Yeah, want to taste you," Leo said, dipping his head to slide his mouth down over Nick's cock.

Nick closed his eyes and let his head fall back, overwhelmed. Leo's mouth was warm and hot, sliding down his length before his tongue dragged against the head. Nick shivered.

He reached out, wanting to touch Leo, to anchor himself, and Leo let out a happy little noise when Nick slipped a hand into his hair.

"You like that?" Nick whispered, combing through it.

Leo hummed the affirmative and Nick's stomach tightened, the vibrations making the intensity ramp up even higher.

Fuck, he wasn't going to last at all.

He gripped the duvet in his fist, panting as Leo sped up, the wet sounds of his mouth filling the air. All Nick could do was hold on and hope he didn't come embarrassingly quickly.

Nick whimpered when Leo pulled off, the air cool against his spit-slicked cock. Leo rubbed his thigh soothingly. "You're close, yeah?"

Nick nodded.

"Good. Where do you want to come?"

"Uhh, what are you good with?" Nick rasped, combing his hand through Leo's soft, silky hair, making it stand on end.

Leo thumbed over the slit in the head of Nick's cock, making his eyes briefly roll back in his head. "I'd love if you came in my mouth but I'm fine with anywhere else on my body."

"Mouth," Nick choked out. "Mouth is good."

"Then stop holding out on me. I want your cum." Leo gave him a big grin before he lowered his mouth over Nick's cock.

The encouragement was nice but Nick doubted he could hold back for much of anything. Not when he was so close to the edge already. Not when it had been so damn long. Not when he was drunk on Leo's touch and the way he was gently leading Nick toward his release.

"Leo," Nick choked out, thighs shaking as his balls drew up and his stomach tightened.

"Mmm," Leo hummed around him and Nick fell apart, swirling colors going off in his head like fireworks as he came and came.

He was shaking after, panting and sheened with sweat. Leo took a drink of water from a bottle on the nightstand, then slid up the bed a moment later, burrowing against him. His skin was cool and Nick reached out, pulling him close.

"Fuck. Thank you."

Chuckling, Leo pressed a kiss to Nick's shoulder. "You liked that?"

Nick gave him a disbelieving look. "Why wouldn't I?"

Leo shrugged and Nick realized he'd barely touched Leo. Maybe he thought Nick viewed this as a *favor* or something.

He rolled over, pressing Leo down against the sheets. "It was amazing," he said huskily.

Nick bent his head and kissed Leo. He responded immediately, winding his arms around Nick's shoulders and opening his mouth. He liked the soft sounds Leo made and the way his body felt when Nick shifted, coaxing Leo to wrap his legs around him.

"Nick," he gasped, arching his hips, his cock hard against Nick's stomach.

The sensation was unfamiliar but *good.*

Still kissing Leo, Nick smoothed a hand across Leo's torso, feeling the soft bumps of his ribcage and the flat planes of his pecs. He rubbed his thumb across Leo's nipple and smiled at the answering shudder.

"Yeah, you like that?" he whispered.

Leo whimpered. "Do it again."

So Nick did it again. He trailed his lips lower, skating over Leo's jaw, the sensation of stubble scraping against his lips sending a tingle through his body.

Despite the orgasm he'd just had, his body responded and he smiled to himself. He licked his thumb and dragged it across Leo's nipple as he kissed his way down his throat, gently biting at the skin.

"Fuck! Nick. God, it's so much."

"Too much?" Nick asked, pulling back to look Leo in the eye.

"Fuck no. Get back here," Leo demanded and Nick chuckled, pressing a kiss to Leo's collarbone before licking a stripe across it.

"Better?" he asked, tweaking his nipple.

"So much fucking better."

Smiling, Nick stretched up to kiss his mouth again.

He allowed his palm to wander across Leo's skin, mapping where he was more or less sensitive, spurred on by Leo's sounds and the way he twisted away from or into the touch.

He found a ticklish spot, making Leo squirm, and laughing, they tried to kiss again, suddenly clumsy.

Nick liked the brush of hair against his palm as he dragged his hand below Leo's navel, the soft texture turning a little coarser farther down.

They both grew serious when Nick took Leo's cock in his hand, liking the slender length and the softness of his skin. He stroked gently, watching the flutter of Leo's eyelashes as he experimented with different strokes.

Leo let out a gasp. "Nick!"

Nick licked his palm, tasting Leo's precum as he got it wet. Leo moaned, a low, long sound that made heat break out on Nick's skin.

"Nick." Leo lifted his hips, urging Nick to stroke faster and harder. "*Fuck.*"

"Do you want me to?" Nick murmured.

"What?" Leo asked hoarsely.

"Do you want me to fuck you?" He pressed his hips to Leo's thigh, letting him feel the rising interest in Nick's cock.

He couldn't remember the last time he'd gotten hard again

so quickly but the feel and taste of Leo were powerful incentives on top of a self-induced drought.

"God. Yes." Leo shifted, dislodging Nick's grip. "I've got lube and condoms here somewhere."

Nick watched him roll over and rummage around in the drawer. He liked the width of Leo's shoulders, the narrowness of his hips, and the lush roundness of his ass.

Leo tossed lube on the bed and Nick reached out, brushing his hand across one of Leo's cheeks.

He let out a little noise. "God, I *better* have some condoms in here," he muttered, rummaging a little harder.

Nick smiled. "We can always go out and get some."

Leo shot a glance over his shoulder, his expression skeptical. "You'd do that?"

"If you wanted. Or I can get you off another way." Nick shrugged.

He wasn't terribly excited about the thought of the entire town talking about them hooking up, which was exactly what would happen if they went to the drugstore or gas station together. Hell, even if he went alone, there would be talk he was on the market again but he'd do it.

Even though his parents and sister would inevitably find out. Even though *Ford* would hear the gossip. Nick grimaced at that thought but thankfully Leo had turned away, digging through the drawer again.

"Found it!" He held the packet up and waved it around.

Nick grinned. "Yes, but is it expired?"

Leo squinted at the package, then shook his head. "Nope. Good until the middle of next year."

"Perfect."

Leo handed it over and Nick sat up, intending to grab the lube but Leo beat him to it.

"Want to watch while I open myself up?" he asked.

Dumbly, Nick nodded. He would have been happy to do it for Leo but he wasn't going to turn down an opportunity to learn what Leo liked.

Leo shifted until he was on his hands and knees, facing away from Nick. He reached slick fingers behind himself, teasing them between his cheeks.

Nick's mouth went dry at the sight.

"Fuck." Nick had been stroking his cock, idle little touches along the hard shaft.

"Good?" Leo asked and there was a hint of something in his voice, some vulnerability, and Nick scooted closer.

"Yeah," he whispered, getting up on his hands and knees and pressing his lips to Leo's shoulderblade. "That's so hot."

Nick shifted back to get a better view again, but he kept his hand on Leo's body, stroking his skin as he watched Leo tease himself. He smoothed a hand over his side, then down, using his thumb to tug Leo's cheeks apart.

Leo let out a little gasp.

"That okay?" Nick asked.

"Yeah. I—I like you watching me."

"Good," he said huskily. "I like watching you."

He wet his lips, watching Leo slide two fingers inside himself, his body resisting for a split second before it yielded to the intrusion.

For the longest time, Nick watched, transfixed, loving the little shivers and gasps Leo let out when he worked in another finger.

"Put the condom on," Leo rasped, looking over his shoulder at him.

Nick fumbled to find it in the covers, feeling a little clumsy as he tore the packet open and rolled the rubber on. But the way Leo stared at him made him feel like he was doing something right. He stared right back, watching Leo shallowly fuck himself and Nick could feel the pulse of his own need in his cock. Less urgent than it had been before, but equally intense.

"Let me … can I help?" he asked.

Leo dropped his head, shuddering. "Yeah. Fuck."

Nick's hands were shaking when he slicked his fingers. Leo pulled his free and Nick pushed his own in carefully. Leo cried out, making Nick freeze.

"No, no it's good," Leo said with a little gasp. "So good. Yeah. Keep going."

So Nick did. He thrust shallowly at first, worried about hurting Leo, but he seemed to love it, especially when Nick followed his instructions to crook his fingers a little.

When he finally got it right, Leo tightened around him, body trembling, his skin beginning to sheen with sweat. "Fuck, I can't—" Leo said. "I need your dick in me. Please."

Nick carefully pulled his fingers away, going up onto his knees to line up his cock.

"Yeah, do it," Leo said and Nick gripped his hip tightly, fingers sliding a little on his damp skin as he pressed inside slowly.

"Fuck," he whispered when he was all the way in, head swimming at the heat and pressure. The feel of Leo wrapped so tightly around him. "You okay?"

"Yeah, so good. C'mon. Move. I can take it."

"I know," Nick said, pressing a kiss to his shoulder. "But I need to go slow or I'll combust."

Over his shoulder, Leo grinned.

Nick stretched out over Leo's back, bracing a hand on the sheets and pressing his lips to Leo's smiling mouth. "You feel too good," he whispered and Leo sighed, kissing him again.

But the need for more soon won out and Nick began to rock his hips.

Leo went down onto his elbows and everything went hazy after that, the world shrinking to the feel of Leo around and beneath him, the heady tightness of his body and scent of his skin. Nick scattered kisses haphazardly across Leo's shoulder, tasting his sweat, making him gasp and buck and clench around him.

"Stop teasing me," Leo growled eventually and Nick laughed, nipping at his skin. But he straightened, sliding his hands to Leo's narrow hips and driving in harder. Their skin slapped together, loud in the otherwise quiet apartment, and Leo moaned, shivering around him.

"I'm close. Fuck, I'm close." He shifted, getting a hand under himself.

Belatedly, Nick realized he should help out so he reached for Leo's cock. Together, they stroked and a few moments later, Leo went still, letting out a short, sharp cry before he shivered and gasped through his release, coating both their fists.

"Leo," Nick whispered, petting his side, desperate to continue but not sure if it would feel good to him or not.

"Yeah, fuck me through it," Leo rasped.

So Nick did. It only took a few more thrusts before he was coming too, overwhelmed by the clench of Leo's body and the taste of his skin on his lips. He came until his blood was boiling, heat streaking across his skin so fast he'd burst into flames.

He came until he was panting and shaking, fingers pressing so hard into Leo's skin they would leave marks—at least temporarily—and he had to close his eyes when everything went white.

CHAPTER ELEVEN

The air was cool on Leo's skin so he wrestled the blanket up over them both. Every square inch of his body buzzed with contentment as he burrowed closer to Nick.

Nick's eyes were closed and his chest rose and fell with quick inhales and exhales.

A part of Leo was tempted to ask him what this meant. What Nick wanted now. But he bit his lip, afraid if he pushed, he'd ruin it. When he'd staged the little moment with Jett earlier, he'd hoped he'd get Remy's attention and help Jett out.

He'd never imagined this. Never dreamed Nick would respond this way or admit he wanted Leo. And okay, Leo was biased but that had been fucking *great* sex, especially for a first time.

He smoothed a hand across Nick's chest, exploring the sprinkle of dark hair there. *Hot.* He could feel questions crowding against his tongue, struggling to burst forth, and he bit his lip, trying to enjoy the moment and bask in the feel of Nick's arms around him.

He smelled good. Like a warm, crackling fire and spices and a sweet richness that made Leo want to lick him all over.

"Ugh, I should clean up," Nick said with a low groan. "I need to get this condom off and I'm lying in the wet spot and it's not pleasant."

"Yeah, sorry about that."

"No, don't apologize." Nick pressed his lips to Leo's hair. "This is nice."

Leo propped himself on one elbow. "Just nice?"

"The sex was phenomenal. Lying here with you would be amazing too if we weren't such a mess."

"Fair," Leo said, sitting up with a grin. "I can accept that. Want to shower with me?" It would be a super tight fit in the tiny shower, but it would be totally worth it.

"I'll borrow a cloth, if you don't mind. I should head home soon," Nick said with a sigh as he sat upright too.

"Yeah? You could stay, if you wanted," Leo offered, though he suspected Nick would say no.

Nick gave Leo a look he couldn't read, then shook his head, settling his hand on Leo's thigh. "I can't. Gotta get home to Jelly."

"Would you otherwise?" Leo asked, because he was a stupid masochist like that.

Nick hesitated, then shook his head. "No. And it's not that I don't *want* to. A part of me does. I just …"

"You're not ready?" Leo supplied when it was clear Nick wasn't going to finish.

"That," Nick said. "And, honestly, I feel like I've muddied the waters enough. I was supposed to be finding dates for you. Not having sex with you. This was incredibly unprofessional of me."

Leo bit his lip. Fuck. He'd been afraid of this.

"Do you regret it?" Leo asked quietly, staring down at the rumpled sheets.

"No. Of course not. I just—I don't want to get your hopes up, Leo. I know you're a romantic and I like that about you. But I—"

"You can't offer me what I want."

"No." Nick's mouth turned down. "I'm not ready."

"Hey, it's okay," Leo said softly. "I'm a big boy. I can handle it. This is just some casual sex."

Nick winced. "I'd like to think it's a little more than that."

"Well, friends with benefits, anyway," Leo said with a forced grin. "I get the difference. I really do. You're not offering me commitment."

Nick sighed. "No matter what you call it, casual isn't my style."

Leo raised an eyebrow. "Sounds to me like you're the one who isn't clear about what you want."

"No, it's not that. Or, maybe it is. I don't know." Nick's expression turned conflicted. "You're—you're the second person I've ever had sex with, Leo. That's … that's not something I take lightly."

"Oh," Leo whispered. He'd known Nick and Nicole had been together for a long time and that Nick had been in mourning, but he'd thought there had been someone else when Nick was younger. Or someone since Nicole's death. "Does it matter that I'm a guy?"

Nick shook his head. "No. The sex was amazing and I—I liked being with you. That part was perfect. I … I need some time to process it all. To really think about my future."

Leo frowned, but nodded. "Yeah, okay."

"I'm sorry." Nick said and he truly did look sorry. "I feel like I hurt you or let you down or led you on …"

Leo managed a faint smile. "We both know I'm a hopeless romantic, Nick. Maybe—maybe for a minute I let myself think this was something more but you've been nothing but honest with me."

"You're such a good person, Leo," Nick said thickly.

Gah, why did that feel like there was a but there? A polite brush-off. But Nick remained silent.

"Thanks," Leo said, eventually, long past the point of awkwardness.

"I should, uh, go clean up," Nick said tightly.

"Bathroom's down the hall," Leo told him. "Help yourself to anything you need. Just, um, be careful. The door tends to stick."

"Sure. Thanks."

Leo stared blankly at the wall next to the bed until Nick returned and began dressing. When he was done, Leo stood, pasting a smile on his face. "Um, I'm going to go shower. You want me to walk you out?"

"No." Nick cleared his throat. "I can—I can let myself out."

They stood there, staring at each other for several long moments before Nick wet his lips and stepped forward. "Thank you."

"Yeah, you're welcome," Leo said, because what the fuck else was there to say? He'd had the best sex of his life and now the dude was walking out. And Leo couldn't even be fucking mad at him because he got why Nick was feeling weird and awkward. Why he was probably feeling guilty and conflicted.

He hugged Nick goodbye because he hated the miserable, hangdog look on Nick's face. Nick let out a shuddering sigh, burrowing against him for a moment before he pulled away.

Nick opened his mouth like he was going to say something—probably apologize or something stupid like that—so Leo kissed him. It was short and tinged with the flavor of regret but he kissed Nick in case it was the last time he ever got to do that.

"G'night," Leo said thickly and turned and fled down the hall for the bathroom. A few minutes later, over the rushing of the water, Leo heard Nick's footfalls in the hallway. They stopped outside the door for a moment, then continued on. A moment later, the apartment door closed.

Fuck! Leo leaned his head against the shower wall and burst into tears.

Nick's heart was heavy as he let himself into his home a short while later. He'd screwed that up, hadn't he?

He could smell and taste Leo in his nose and on his skin. He could hear the echo of Leo's desperate little sounds and the feel of his body curled close. Nick could see the hurt in Leo's eyes and his throat thickened.

He'd … he'd hurt Leo. And that was a terrible feeling. Earlier, as they'd talked behind The White Elephant, Nick had only meant to reassure Leo he was wanted.

And he was.

Having sex with Leo certainly hadn't made Nick want him any less.

It had only made him want Leo *more.* He'd wanted to stay curled up in Leo's bed. He'd wanted to pull Leo even closer, kiss him until he was breathless and laughing. Kiss him until their eyes drooped and they grew too tired to kiss anymore.

He wanted to sleep beside Leo and wake him up with breakfast. He wanted to tell Leo to stop looking for anyone else when Nick was *right here*.

But the longer he lay there, the more anxious and guilty he felt. What if it was too soon? What if he wasn't ready?

Nick hung his coat on the peg rail by the door, staring at the empty spots where Nicole's jackets and umbrella had once dangled. He'd had a similar empty spot in his heart for so long. For a while, he'd thought he'd never want to fill it up with someone else's clutter. Someone else's love.

But he'd been wrong. He *did* want it.

It scared him. It scared him to think of letting himself get close to someone. Letting himself open to the idea of love.

He'd put the idea of love in a box and shoved it into the future. To a point where he never thought he'd actually get to. Not shutting himself off from it, but *delaying* it.

But no … he was tricking himself, wasn't he? He was shutting himself off because it was safer and less terrifying than risking being hurt again. Hell, this wasn't even the first time he'd done something like that.

He'd pushed Ford away when he needed a friend the most. He'd turned down dates, walled his heart off … He'd been afraid of letting anyone be close.

"Fuck," Nick whispered and the noise echoed in the empty home.

From the other room, Jelly chirped and he heard the quiet sound of padding feet on the wooden floors as she ran to him. He picked her up and buried his face against her fur, feeling the warm rumble coming from her chest. "What do I do, Jelly?" he whispered.

She didn't answer, of course, so he carried her through the house. But when he could have turned to go into the kitchen to feed her, he went toward the office instead. He slipped inside, clicking on the lamp on his desk.

Jelly squirmed in his arms so he let her jump down, eager to explore the room she was rarely allowed in.

Nick stared at the photographs he'd taken on the trips he and Nicole went on, smiling wistfully at the sight of the waters of Pendleton Bay, sparkling in the summer sun.

He thought of Leo's bio on the matchmaking app. *I love exploring new places and I hope to travel more in the future. I'm a hopeless romantic, looking to find my happily ever after.*

"But it's not easy, Leo," Nick whispered. "Sometimes forever is only a couple of decades."

Nick shook his head because he'd never once, not even in the depths of the worst of his grief, regretted loving Nicole. He'd never regretted the time they'd had. It had been worth it. Every second of it. Even the call from the hospital. Drowning in grief beside her grave, his sister's tight grip the only thing keeping him from collapsing.

He'd never regretted loving Nicole so why was he so fucking resistant to the idea of finding that with someone else?

And while on the surface, Leo might seem like a somewhat unlikely candidate—he was *so* young, so inexperienced at relationships—he filled something inside Nick he couldn't quite explain. Nick felt more alive, more hopeful with Leo around. More like himself than he had in years.

He walked over the shelf of books, tracing his finger across the Morgan Nicola name inked on the spines.

"How do your heroes do it?" Nick whispered. "How do they know when they've found their person?"

Fuck, he was a matchmaker. He'd had a happy marriage for fifteen fucking years. He should know what made for good relationships. Should know when it was right. When the feelings went beyond lust and infatuation, when they held the potential to grow from a tiny kernel of love into something strong and true and *real.*

Nick searched the shelf, looking for a book about a widower finding love again.

He cracked *A Model Husband* open, nose filling with the familiar scent of paper and ink. He skimmed through the text, the details coming back to him as he read.

Nick had always read her books, been one of the first people she sent them to for feedback, and he'd been so fucking proud of her and what she'd created. So in awe of the way she made imaginary people come to life, the way they grew, the way they tugged at his heartstrings.

"I need your help," he whispered. "Please, tell me how I get this right. I don't want to hurt him."

A moment later, Nick paused, reading more slowly.

"How do I know when it's right?" Damien asked, pacing in front of the desk. "When I'm ready to move on?"

Kenzie smiled at him. "You don't. You just have to trust."

Nick closed the book and pressed it against his chest, staring at his reflection in the dark window across the room but not seeing it.

"Is that it?" he asked. "Is it that simple?"

Jelly wound around his ankles, mewing impatiently for food, which wasn't very helpful. But something inside Nick's chest seemed to settle for the first time since he left Leo's apartment and he nodded to himself.

Trust, he thought.

"I can do that," he said aloud. "I can."

CHAPTER TWELVE

"Hey, why the long face?" Joel asked.

Leo glanced up from his laptop with a watery smile. It had been two days since Nick walked out and there hadn't been a peep from him.

Leo shrugged, not wanting to spill his guts in the middle of the bakery. It wasn't super crowded but there were a few people here.

Heath Kelly was here, sipping coffee and doing something on his phone. An elderly couple he didn't recognize was by the counter and a younger guy hung back, staring at the pastries. He was slim with blondish curls, kinda cute, but not cute enough to distract Leo from moping over Nick.

"Just feeling unlucky in love," Leo admitted, glancing back at Joel.

"Aww. Mind if I sit?" The baker's face creased into a worried frown.

"Nope." It was mid-morning and he'd come downstairs to the bakery to work because he was afraid he was going to turn into a weird, depressed hermit staying in his apartment all day. But he was struggling to focus on anything. He needed a distraction.

"So, what happened? I thought you were going on some dates," Joel said quietly.

"Yeah, I was. They're not going well. And, like, I kinda hooked up with someone else who I thought it might go somewhere with and yeah … totally backfired on me." Leo sighed, staring at the half-eaten piece of quiche on the plate. It was delicious but it couldn't compete with the knot in Leo's stomach.

"Backfired how?"

Leo shrugged. "He's not—he's not looking for a relationship."

"Hey, what can I get you?" Cassie asked.

Leo glanced over at the curly-haired guy who stood by the counter now. "Two cinnamon rolls, please."

"I'm sorry," Joel said, his tone sympathetic. "Dating can be hard."

Leo rolled his eyes, settling back in his chair and focusing on Joel again. "Says the man with the perfect relationship."

"Hey, it took me a long time to find someone," Joel pointed out. "I had my share of disappointments."

"Yeah. I dunno. Maybe I made a mistake moving to Christmas Falls."

Joel gave him a horrified look. "No. We can't have you thinking that! Hey, why don't you come over this evening and hang out?"

"With you and Hayden?"

"Well, I know we're not the most exciting people," Joel teased. "And we still have boxes to unpack. But you haven't met our new cat yet! And there's a comfy couch to hang out on while you and Hayden can catch up. I feel like I've been monopolizing his time lately."

"Nah, it's all good," Leo said with a wave of his hand. It was true he and Hayden hadn't hung out much lately but that wasn't Joel's fault. He was busy with the bakery this time of year so he and Hayden tried to spend as much time together as they could when they weren't working. "But I will come over later today, if you're sure that's okay."

"Yeah, of course," Joel said, giving him a warm smile behind his ginger beard. "We'd love to have you. I'll let Hayden know."

"Sounds good." Leo offered a tentative smile. "I mean, I'll be fine. I'm just feeling mopey and a little lonely and unappreciated. Part of it is probably the holidays. It—it's hard being single this time of year, you know?"

"I know." Joel stood and patted his shoulder. "But you do have friends here."

"Thanks. I appreciate that. It means a lot to me," he said honestly.

"Good. Now, I should get back to work. Those gingerbread men don't decorate themselves."

Leo smiled. "You never know! When I was a kid, there was a book at my grandma's house I loved. I think it belonged to my mom when she was little. There were these little gingerbread bears who came to life and helped with the holiday preparations. They cleaned the kitchen and decorated the tree and knitted a sweater or something. It was super cute."

"It *sounds* cute. Hmm, maybe I should do some bears this year ..." Joel walked off, muttering to himself about bear ears.

Leo smiled faintly, ducking his head and returning his attention to the laptop in front of him, the jingle of the bell as someone left the shop a familiar background noise.

"So you did the complete opposite of what I suggested and it backfired on you?" Hayden said, later that evening.

Leo, who was lying on the floor of Joel and Hayden's new living room, petting their new black cat, Coal, sighed. "Kind of."

Hayden stepped closer, staring down at him and Coal. "I told you to give the other guys a real chance and, instead, you slept with Nick!"

"Umm," Leo said, pretending to be fascinated by the vintage light fixture above his head. "No?"

"No to which one?" Hayden put his hands on his hips, his expression sharpening to a glare.

"I mean, I did try to give the other guys a real chance," Leo pointed out. "Then I *selflessly* helped Jett get together with his dude!"

"And you slept with Nick."

Leo grimaced. "I did do that, yes."

"And he pulled a fuck and duck on you?"

Leo covered his face with his hands. "He didn't fuck and duck on me," he muttered, his words a little muffled.

"Well, what the hell else do you call it?"

Leo rolled onto his side, then sat up, trying not to squish the cat. "I'm the first person he's had sex with since his wife died, Hayden. The first man he's ever had sex with. He's allowed to be a little confused and need a little time to get his head in order."

"He is," Hayden said, plopping onto the floor in front of him and dragging Coal onto his lap. "He's allowed to do that for sure. But saying he wants you and claiming what he did was unprofessional, then saying he doesn't do casual … that's a lot of mixed messages, Leo."

"I know." Leo sighed, his shoulders slumping.

"And it's been a couple of days and you haven't heard from him," Hayden pointed out, rubbing between the cat's ears.

"Uuugh." Leo slumped backwards, staring at the ceiling again. "I know."

"Why don't you take a little break?" Hayden said softly.

"From life? Tell me how because that sounds amazing."

"Well, I meant from dating. *Life* seems a little melodramatic."

"That's me," Leo muttered. "The melodramatic dateless wonder."

"Oh my God." Hayden let out a huff. "You are fucking ridiculous."

"It was the best sex of my life!" Leo protested. "I am allowed to be a little ridiculous."

"I think there's some recency bias there, but sure."

A quiet rapping noise filled the air and Leo rolled his head to see Joel holding out a plate of something. "I apologize for interrupting but would fresh pumpkin cinnamon rolls be a welcome addition to this pity party?"

"Hell yes," Leo said. "I might even get off the floor for that."

Joel laughed and crossed the room, setting the plate on the rug between Leo and Hayden. "No need. I'm happy to do a delivery."

"You're the best," Hayden said with a sigh as he reached for one.

Coal stretched out, his nose quivering as he sniffed the pastry. Joel scooped him up, holding him like a baby.

"You really are," Leo agreed, rolling onto his side and staring up at Hayden's handsome baker and their adorable new pet. "A prince among men."

"Nah, just a baker with a knack for comfort food," Joel said with a twinkle in his eyes.

Leo stuffed a bite of the rich, soft pastry in his mouth. "I'd marry you if I could," he muttered around the mouthful.

"Excuse me!" Hayden protested. "You will not."

Leo swallowed. "That's why I said *if I could*. Sadly, you don't want to be sister wives."

Hayden glowered. "I'd say get your *own* man but that's what got you into this mess in the first place!"

"You aren't very nice to me," Leo pointed out, scooping up a dollop of cream cheese threatening to slide off the roll.

"I'm letting you mope on my living room floor and my boyfriend is feeding you fresh baked goods. I'm very nice."

"If you were really nice, you'd let me borrow him," Leo teased.

Hayden made an outraged noise and Leo giggled, his mood already lifting. Maybe it was the baked goods. Maybe it was having friends like this he could vent to, but he couldn't stay mopey for long.

"I'll be fine," he said with a sigh. "Eventually. I'm going to let Nick know I'm taking a break from the matchmaking until the holidays are over and focusing on making friends in the area for a while."

"Sounds like a good plan," Hayden said. "And I'm sorry things got so messy with Nick."

"Meh." Leo shrugged. "Story of my life."

Nick,

I understand why you needed some space after the other night. But I think we should keep things professional going forward.

For my sake, I think I'm going to take a break from matchmaking until the new year. I need to clear my head. Thanks for how hard you've worked to try to find me someone and I'll let you know when I'm ready to start dating again.

I wish you the best. Enjoy the holidays.

Your friend, Leo

p.s. If the website needs anything, please reach out via email. I think phone convos aren't the best for me right now.

With a pounding heart, Leo hit *Send* on the email, closed his laptop, and stood.

He'd been thinking about Hayden's words since last night and although it sucked to have to step back from dating and talking to Nick, it was the right choice. No point in him moping around. He was going to take a little break, enjoy the holidays the best he could, and he'd worry about dating when he was ready.

He'd put too much pressure on himself to find someone quickly. That was all.

With that done, he decided to take a mid-morning coffee and pastry break. Otherwise, he'd obsessively stalk his email inbox, waiting for a response.

The bakery downstairs was warm and fragrant with spices and baking bread when he slipped through the back door into the hallway. Joel's office door was open and Hayden waved at him as he passed. He waved distractedly back, a phone pressed between his ear and shoulder as he wrote something down.

Leo helped himself to some coffee, then got in line behind a couple of people.

Across the room, Heath Kelly waved, on his way out the door. "Have a good day, Leo!"

"You too!" Leo waved back and the bell tinkled as Heath walked out.

They'd been running into each other a lot lately. Heath seemed to stop into the bakery right around the time Leo took his mid-morning breaks.

Leo chatted with a couple of people while he waited in line, listening to an older woman talk about how someone had cleared the sidewalk for her following a dusting of snow they'd gotten recently.

"Seems to be going around," another woman said. "There have been all kinds of good deeds happening around town."

Leo smiled, a little of the weight he'd been carrying on his shoulders melting away. The talk with Hayden and Joel last night *had* helped and he felt better now that he'd sent the email.

It sucked. He missed Nick. Missed talking to him.

But there were great things about living here too and he needed to focus on the positives and enjoy the holidays as much as possible.

"Oh, hey!" Cassie said when he reached the front of the line. "There's a package for you!"

"Yeah?" His mail was mixed in with the bakery's when it arrived, and Joel had hung a little post box on the wall of the stairwell leading up to his apartment. There was no good place to leave a package though, so they held them in Joel's office until he picked them up. "Probably something from my mom. I've tried to keep the late-night shopping to a minimum lately."

Cassie laughed. "No, not that kind of package. It's something someone hand delivered. It's tagged with your name though!"

"Oh." Leo tilted his head. "Well, that's weird. Wonder who it's from."

"No idea. We got busy at the bakery this morning and all of a sudden, I turned around and saw it on the counter. I asked around but no one fessed up to dropping it off."

"Mysterious! I'm intrigued."

"Me too!" Cassie said. "Be right back with it."

Leo waited patiently for her to return, then ordered a pastry to go. He juggled it, a cup of coffee, and the box on the way up to his apartment, too curious to wait and see what was inside.

He munched on the cranberry nut puff pastry tree as he sliced the box open with a pair of scissors. Inside the plain brown box, he found some candy-cane striped paper. He peeled it back to reveal a small Lego snowman set, a little package of chocolates from Jingle Bites Chocolate Haven—a shop in town—and a simple origami kit with paper and instructions to make snowflakes and Christmas trees. There was also a note.

Leo picked it up and read it carefully.

Leo,

Welcome to Christmas Falls! My elves told me you're having a rough time lately. Sometimes the holidays can be tough but I hope these small gifts put a smile on your face and take your mind off your woes!

Happy Holidays, Your Secret Santa

Leo smiled. What a sweet gesture. Who on earth was it from though? His first thought was Joel and Hayden but it wasn't either of their styles. Hayden's love language was sarcasm and tough love and Joel's was baked goods.

Had Cassie done it and made up the story about it being from someone else? Had Nick sent it?

God a part of Leo wanted it to be Nick but no, he had seen Nick's handwriting and it looked *nothing* like this.

With a shrug, Leo popped one of the chocolates in his mouth, moaning as it melted on his tongue. Well that was delicious. He was definitely going to have to go check the shop out soon.

And he'd put the Lego snowman together tonight while he watched the Otters lose.

Later that evening, Nick read Leo's email three times, feeling worse with every pass he made. Fuck.

Fuck, fuck, fuck.

He had royally screwed up, hadn't he?

The other night, Nick had been filled with determination to move forward with his life and let Leo know he wanted to date him but he'd needed some time to get his thoughts in order and now … Yeah, now Leo thought Nick had blown him off.

And he was giving up on dating completely.

Which, Nick didn't hate the idea of Leo taking a break from dating other people. But Nick needed to get his shit together and show Leo he was serious about dating *him*.

Because Nick wasn't sure he could think of the guy he'd held in his arms the other night as just a *friend*. No, Leo felt like someone Nick wanted to get to know better. Someone who could be a very important part of Nick's future if he was lucky.

And now he was hurt because of the way Nick had acted.

"Oh, Jelly, I'm not very bright, am I?" Nick muttered.

She chirruped and kneaded his thigh, her razor-sharp claws sinking into the denim and pricking his skin. He flinched, but didn't dislodge her. He probably deserved worse.

With a sigh, Nick navigated away from the message. Okay, he'd definitely reply to Leo's email later but first, he needed to talk to his sister.

"No shit," she said with a snort several hours later as he slumped at her kitchen table. "I could have told you that weeks ago."

"What?" he sputtered. "But how did you …"

"Oh, come on. It was so obvious you were interested in Leo." She smirked. "God, I could see it at the Parade of Lights."

"Am I the only one who didn't know?" he asked helplessly.

She shrugged. "I don't know, there's probably someone deep in the jungles of the Amazon or high in the Himalayas who didn't notice, but you were broadcasting your interest in him pretty loudly."

Nick rolled his eyes. "Well someone could have *told* me."

"I didn't think you were ready," she said softly. "I thought you needed more time."

"So did I!" he admitted.

"Are you sure you still don't?"

Nick sighed. "I'm sure if I don't *try* with Leo, I'll regret it. The sex was amazing and—"

"That doesn't mean you're ready for a relationship," she pointed out.

"I know." He wrapped his hands around his mug of peppermint tea. "But I—I care about him. He makes me feel alive and excited about life again. He makes me feel like it's worth risking my heart again."

"Oh, Nick."

"What?"

She reached out and squeezed his arm. "I'm glad. I'm glad you feel that way. I just—be careful, okay?"

"Careful of what?"

"Leo. No one deserves to have someone toy with their feelings."

"I didn't—well, I didn't *mean* to toy with him."

"I know. I know it wouldn't be intentional. But take it slow, okay? If you confess your feelings, he might be willing to give you another shot, but don't just immediately hop into bed with him again. Take your *time* to get to know him this time. *Date* him."

"Hmm," Nick said. That was good advice and he wasn't opposed to it. "Like ask him to dinner?"

Heather shook her head, a pained expression crossing her face. "You know, I never knew how dense you were when it comes to romance. I had no idea it was all Nicole who made your relationship seem like a fairy tale."

Nick let out an outraged noise of protest. "Hey! That's not fair. I was a great husband!"

She grinned. "You have to admit, she made it easy on you."

"She did," he acknowledged.

"So, step up your game this time!" Heather said with a laugh. "You're a *matchmaker*. You have all of the info about what Leo is looking for right in front of you. If you're serious about winning Leo back, be as objective as you can and put those skills to good use. Romance him!"

"Romance him," Nick mouthed.

"Oh for God's sake," she muttered, then raised her voice. "Edie! Come here. We need reinforcements. My brother is useless and he needs all of the help we can give him so he doesn't completely fuck up the rest of his life!"

Under the table, Nick kicked her shin and she yelped, kicking him back.

Nick grinned into his mug of tea, feeling hopeful. With Edie and Heather helping, surely he couldn't screw this up.

"Hey there, fancy meeting you here."

Leo glanced up to see Heath Kelly, the Hallmark movie heart-throb, smiling at him. "Oh, hi." He smoothed down his hair.

He'd come downstairs for a mid-morning break from work to get a pastry and some coffee, which was becoming a routine of his. Heath usually stopped by around the same time and they kept running into each other.

"So, how's work going? You're a web developer, right?" Heath asked.

"Oh, pretty good," Leo said, flattered he'd remembered. "You know, the same ol' same ol' most days, but it pays the bills." He laughed awkwardly. "Not that you know what that's like. I'm sure being an actor is a lot more exciting."

Heath leaned in. "I don't know. Some days it can be tedious."

"Yeah?" Leo asked, curious. There were a few people ahead of them in line so maybe Heath wouldn't mind chatting about it.

"Well, sometimes it's a lot of standing around. Two minutes of shooting, then forty-five to set up a slightly different angle."

"Interesting." Leo took a sip of his coffee.

"God no. Horribly tedious."

Leo chuckled. "Okay, fair. But the premieres must be glamorous."

"Yes. Although after, my feet and my face hurt."

"Face?"

"From smiling." He flashed a perfect, even white smile Leo's way.

"Tragic."

"Very," Heath said, stepping a little closer, his expression turning serious. "Honestly, I'm lucky. I love what I do. But yeah, it's not all glitz and glam."

"That's fair." No job was.

"Hey, Leo, what can I get you this morning?"

He glanced across the counter to see Cassie grinning at him. "Oh! Sorry. I was distracted. Um …" He scanned the bakery and his jaw nearly dropped at the new addition. "Oh my God. I have to try one of those gingerbread cinnamon rolls. That sounds *incredible.*"

"They're killer," Cassie said. "New addition to the menu this season. My idea, actually, if I can brag a little." She polished her nails on her apron.

"Awesome!" Leo brightened. "That's cool that Joel's putting your recipes on the menu."

"He's a great boss! Couldn't ask for better." She slid one of the rolls onto a plate. "Want it warmed up?"

"Yes please."

She glanced between Leo and Heath. "Together or separate?"

"Separate," Leo said as Heath settled a hand on his waist, leaning closer. "Together."

"Oh, you don't have to," Leo said, surprised and a little confused. "I've got it."

"I know I don't have to." Heath smiled at him. "But I'd like to, if you don't mind."

"I, uhh, no, that's fine," Leo managed. Was … was Heath flirting with him?

He studied Heath as he ordered a slice of vegan roasted red pepper, spinach, and tomato quiche.

Like Nick, he was … tall, dark, and handsome too. With thick wavy brown hair and stunning features, he *belonged* in movies. Hell, on paper he was better looking than Nick. But he didn't make Leo's stomach go all fluttery.

After Heath paid, he took his plate, and Leo's, then turned to face him.

"So, I've definitely noticed you around, Leo," Heath said, his gaze sweeping appreciatively over Leo's body. "I'd love to get to know you more."

"Yeah?"

"*Absolutely*."

Leo hesitated. "Well, unless you have somewhere you need to be right now, we could start with a quick bite? We could share a table while we enjoy our treats and coffee."

He had work to do today but as long as he got it finished by the deadline tomorrow, they didn't care when he did it.

Heath flashed him a brilliant smile. "Sure. Sounds great."

They took seats at the tiny table, shifting their chairs until they were side by side to accommodate a mother with a stroller at a nearby table.

Leo sat and Heath touched his shoulder. "I'm going to grab some coffee. You want a top-up on yours?"

"Nah, I'm good," Leo said. "Thanks."

Heath turned to go but not before he looked Leo up and down again, his gaze lingering, a smile crossing his face as he turned away.

Huh. It was flattering to have a movie star look at him like he was as tasty as Joel's baked goods.

It felt like cool, soothing aloe slathered on his scorched ego.

Having sex with Nick had been a mistake. Leo should've known Nick wasn't ready. And that was … that was okay. Nick should take all of the time he needed. But Leo definitely deserved more.

When Heath returned, they struck up an easy conversation. He seemed like a nice person, though a little more physical than Leo liked a guy to be—putting his hand on Leo's knee a lot—but he was handsome and funny and charming and frankly, Leo was bored stiff.

Leo *should* be gobbling up the attention but something about it felt … wrong.

Fuck.

Maybe he wasn't ready right now either but also, Heath was laying it on pretty thick. Ohh, maybe *he* was the Secret Santa.

"Are you my Secret Santa?" Leo blurted out.

A puzzled look crossed Heath's face before he leaned in, smirking. "Do you want me to be?"

"Uhh, well, I mean, someone delivered a package the other day with a bunch of little gifts in it that made me smile."

He'd finished the Lego snowman and set it up on his dresser in his bedroom, then folded snowflakes and trees to make a garland to hang on the wall in his living room behind the couch.

Heath shook his head. "No, wasn't me. I wouldn't mind making you smile though."

"Am I … am I reading this the right way?" Leo blurted out.

Heath smiled, reaching for his coffee. "Well, how are you reading this?"

"That you're interested in me."

Heath sat back in his chair. "I'm very interested in you. I'm a little concerned it took you this long to figure it out though."

"Well, I didn't want to assume … and that's uh, flattering," Leo said, rubbing his neck. "But are you looking to date anyone seriously?"

Heath winced and sat forward. "I'm not looking for anything serious, no. Just … maybe some fun for a bit? Not a one-night stand but an ongoing hookup while I'm in town? Casual but fun, you know?"

"Yeahhh," Leo said with a sigh. "I'm not sure that's going to work for me. I kinda—there's kinda someone else I'm into."

Heath frowned. "Is he interested in you?"

"Not as much as I'd like."

"Well, then maybe you should think about—"

"I'm sorry to interrupt your date, Leo, but there's something you need to know."

Leo blinked, sure he was imagining the familiar voice but when he glanced up, Nick stood nearby, clutching a bouquet of flowers.

"What? What the hell are *you* doing here?" Leo sputtered, rising to his feet.

Nick smiled. "Romancing you."

Leo blinked, unexpected anger rising up. "You—fu—

fureaking walked out of my apartment the other night and said you weren't ready!"

"I know." Nick grimaced. "I needed a few days to get my thoughts together."

"You let me think you didn't want me, Nick!" he whispered, aware of how quiet the bakery had gone and the people staring intently at them.

"I know." Nick looked miserable. "I did. And I'm sorry. I screwed up. I know I did, Leo. But I—I want you to know I care about you. I want to date you."

"I told you I was taking a break from dating," he said weakly.

Nick glanced at Heath who was looking at Leo and Nick with rapt attention. "Uhh, were you?"

"Yes! This was—um, okay, so maybe *Heath* was interested but I was about to tell him I only wanted to be friends."

"It's true." Heath let out a long-suffering sigh. "I could feel the rejection coming."

"Why is that?" Nick asked softly, looking at Heath. "Why didn't you want to date him?"

"Well, he's not interested in dating me," Leo pointed out. "He was only into the idea of casually hooking up, which *you of all people* should know is not what I want!"

"Fuck." Nick took a step forward. "I'm sorry, Leo. I regret that I didn't stay and talk to you the other night."

Leo nodded.

"Unfortunately, I can't undo the past. But if you'll give me a chance, I'd like to show you I can do better. I want to see if we have a future together."

"Good line," Heath said softly.

Leo was tempted to laugh but he couldn't look away from Nick's beautiful brown eyes. He looked so hopeful. So determined.

"Let me take you out on some dates," Nick continued. "Let me *show* you we could be good together."

Leo hesitated, biting his lip. "You were supposed to be matching me with someone else."

"I was," Nick agreed, holding out the flowers. "But I don't want you to meet anyone else. I want you to fall in love with me. I want you to see you're my perfect match."

Damn it, that was a good line too.

Out of the corner of his eye, he could see Heath nodding approvingly.

Leo sighed, reaching out to take the bouquet Nick was offering. The flowers were gorgeous. Leo spotted red and white roses and white lilies, with some ferns, but he didn't have a clue what the other half of them were. Just knew they were dramatic and unusual, in shades of red, white, and green with little red ornament bulbs and white twiggy things scattered throughout.

A stunning bouquet. Nick had gone all-out.

But as Leo looked into Nick's eyes again, it wasn't the showy flowers tugging at his heart. It was the sincerity in his gaze.

Wary but hopeful, Leo made his decision.

"Right now, I'm agreeing to *one* date," he said, narrowing his eyes. "And you better impress me, Mr. Matchmaker."

CHAPTER THIRTEEN

Unfortunately, setting up the date was harder than Nick had anticipated. Leo had a meeting in Chicago so he was gone from Christmas Falls for a few days. It gave Nick more time to plan but also, more time to worry about how it would all go over.

He was anxious as he texted Leo to tell him he was outside the back entrance to the bakery.

Be down in a sec flashed on his screen a moment later.

Nick tried not to fidget as he waited for Leo to arrive. "Hi," he said when the door swung open, knowing he was acting over-eager but not caring.

Leo smiled. "Hi." He sounded a little breathless and he bit his lip. "Do you mind coming up for a few? I know we have mysterious plans this afternoon and evening, but I need like five minutes to finish getting ready. My Zoom meeting went a little longer than I hoped."

"Sure, no problem," Nick said, tucking his phone in his pocket. "We've got time."

Not a ton of time. But enough.

"Thanks." Leo smiled as he held the door open for Nick. "So, um, how are you?"

"I'm—I'm good," Nick said, hating how awkward they were now.

Leo had been quiet since Nick ambushed him at the bakery and broke up the moment between Leo and Heath.

God, he could have missed his chance. What if Leo had said yes to Heath? What if he'd said no to Nick? He had to get it right today. He *had* to.

"So, are you going to give me any hints about what we're doing tonight?" Leo asked teasingly as he turned to climb the stairs.

Nick laughed, trying not to stare at Leo's ass in the dark jeans he wore. Tried not to think about what Leo's body looked like under his clothes. What he felt like in Nick's arms.

Nick cleared his throat. "No. No hints except for what I already gave you."

"Dress warmly in comfortable clothing and practical shoes that can get dirty. And plan to eat a snack on the way," Leo parroted back.

"Yep," Nick said, grinning as they reached the landing at the top of the stairs.

"Gah. This is driving me crazy!" Leo said. "I've spent the past few days wondering what the hell you have planned."

"Only one way to find out," Nick reminded him with a wink.

"True." Leo pushed open the door to his apartment. "Make yourself comfortable."

Nick leaned against the wall and unzipped his coat as he looked around Leo's apartment.

The living room was small and cozy with a TV stand, TV, comfortable-looking couch, along with a miniscule table and two tiny chairs.

"How on earth did Joel ever fit at that table?" Nick asked, mystified.

Leo chuckled as he took a seat on the couch. "I wondered that too. I'm not surprised he and Hayden bought a house quickly. This place is tiny for a single person. I can't imagine two people living here."

"Hey. You're still working from the couch too," Nick said with a frown as Leo picked up his laptop from the coffee table.

He shrugged, staring at his screen. "Yeah. Haven't had a chance to go check out those shops you mentioned."

"We could go on our next date," Nick offered. "That would be fun."

Typing something, Leo shrugged. "That's assuming you get a second date."

"True." Suitably chastised, Nick grimaced. "I shouldn't get ahead of myself."

Leo glanced up, his expression conflicted. "It isn't that I don't want this, Nick. The problem is that I want it so much it scares me."

"It scares you or you don't trust me?" Nick asked softly.

"I …" Leo winced. "I'm scared I *can't* trust you. You were so adamant about not being ready to date, then … then you got jealous of Jett."

"I wasn't jealous of Jett," he protested. "And you said there was nothing going on between you!"

"There wasn't! But let's be honest, Nick, you only *acted* like you wanted me after you saw me get close to him. And you got all weird about Heath Kelly too."

"You said that wasn't a date either!"

"It wasn't!"

"Leo, do you think I only want you when there's a chance you could be with someone else?"

"Honestly? A little bit."

Nick sighed. That was … fair. He'd royally screwed this whole situation up. "I get why it came across that way. Look, I showed up at the bakery the other day intending to text you and ask you if you had time to come down and have a coffee break with me. I was going to treat you to coffee and a pastry and give you the flowers. I intended to apologize and see if you wanted to date. That was already the plan before I saw you with Heath."

"I get that. But you've been blowing hot and cold with me for weeks, Nick," Leo said softly. "I was willing to give you time. I understood why this was a big shift for you. But you walking out after we had sex and telling me you weren't ready … that *hurt.* And so did not hearing from you after. So forgive me if I feel a little bit wary about trusting you know what you want right now."

"That's a good point," Nick conceded. "And I am sorry. I regret the way I acted after we had sex. I want the opportunity to show you I'm genuinely remorseful."

"I don't *need* lavish apology gifts," Leo said, gesturing to the bouquet of flowers on the coffee table.

They'd held up remarkably well. They should, for what Nick had paid. But mostly he was glad Leo was enjoying them.

"You don't mind them, do you?" Nick asked.

Leo gave him a crooked little smile. "No. I'm just saying that's not the most important part. What I need is to know you're going to follow through on what you say. I need to know I can *trust* you. That you're reliable and ready for what I want."

"That's fair," Nick said. Because it was. It was more than reasonable. He took off his wet boots, then skirted around the coffee table and dropped to both knees so he could look Leo in the eye.

Leo blinked, clearly confused. Nick reached out, gently taking his hand.

"I've handled this badly," Nick admitted. "And I know it seems like I—like I changed my mind very quickly but I *am* sincere."

"What changed for you?"

Nick rubbed his thumb across Leo's knuckles. "I went home and I thought about what I wanted. I thought about you and how I felt about moving on from Nicole and …" He laughed softly. "I found one of her books. It was about a widower finding love again and I flipped through it, trying to find the scene where he had this blinding realization about how he'd know when it was right to move on. And I had it built up in my head as this big moment in the story but it turned out to be very simple."

"Yeah?" Leo tilted his head, his expression curious. "What was it?"

"It boils down to trust," Nick said simply. "I need to trust myself this is right. That I'm ready. And I need to *show* you. You don't have to take my word for it but I'd like if you gave me a real shot at proving it."

Leo smiled softly. "I can do that."

"Good."

"And I, uhm, have a confession to make," Leo said.

Nick arched an eyebrow. "Yeah?"

"Yeah. I think I read that book."

"You've read Nicole's books?" Nick asked, surprised.

"Well, I am sure it'll come as a huge shock to you, but I *am* a hopeless romantic," Leo said drily. "I read romance books."

"No, that part doesn't surprise me," Nick said with a small laugh. "I just didn't realize you knew her pen name or read her books."

He shrugged. "Well, I usually read queer romance but the other day, I went to Season's Readings. They had a cute little display of holiday-themed queer romances but after I found a few new titles to buy, I was wandering around trying to figure out what else they had available and I saw the picture and little write-up of Nicole."

"She was a local. They were proud of her success," Nick explained.

"They should be!" Leo said. "It's amazing. But I—I flipped through the little display of her books and I picked one up. I think it might be the one you were talking about. With Damien and Kenzie, right?"

"Yeah," Nick said, surprised. "*A Model Husband*."

Leo slipped a hand behind the sofa pillow, pulling it out. "I finished it last night. Bawled my eyes out, too."

He handed the book to Nick who stared down at the familiar cover in shock. "Oh."

"Nicole was a hell of a writer."

"She was," Nick agreed. He flipped through the pages for a moment, then looked at Leo. "And I love that you found the same book and read it. Because maybe you can understand how it helped me get some perspective."

"It does," Leo said softly.

Nick set the book down. "But as much as I loved my life with Nicole, I want to think about my future now, Leo. You don't have to promise me anything yet. But I hope you'll be in it. Let me show you I'm sincere and that I can do better."

"Sounds good to me." Leo smiled, squeezing Nick's hand, then let go. "But, let me get this email sent and I'll be ready to go."

"Sounds good." Nick stood with a groan. Jesus, he was getting too damn old to kneel for that long.

Leo shot him an amused smile over the top of his laptop, then closed it. "Okay. Email sent. I'm going to pee before we go. But I swear, I'm ready otherwise." He stood.

"You're fine," Nick said, resisting the urge to reach out and pull Leo close as he brushed past. "We're okay on time."

Nick paced the tiny living room as Leo used the bathroom, but after the toilet flushed and the water ran, he heard a rattle coming from down the hall but no sign of Leo.

"Uhh, Nick," Leo called out a moment later. "We might have a problem."

"What's that?" Nick asked, walking toward the bathroom door.

"I think I'm stuck."

"Gah. Thanks again for the rescue," Leo said a short while later as Nick pulled his truck out onto Blitzen Street. "*So* embarrassing."

"Happy to come to the rescue any time you need it," Nick said lightly.

It had taken a combination of Leo putting his shoulder to the door and Nick tugging with all his might but they'd finally gotten the bathroom door unstuck.

"Why haven't you said something to Joel about fixing it?" Nick asked as they passed the Christmas Falls Festival headquarters.

"Oh." Leo laughed softly. "It wasn't bad at all when I moved in but it's gotten a lot worse lately. It's an older building, so maybe its settling a little? Or I take too long of showers or something and the wood swells from the humidity? I don't know. But the bakery is sooo busy at the holidays and I don't want to bug Joel. I figured I'd talk to him about it in January and since I live alone, I usually leave the door open."

But he'd been trying to be polite with Nick in his apartment and not make it weird by peeing with the door open. Instead Nick had needed to rescue him from being trapped in the bathroom. That was so much less weird.

He stifled a groan.

"Got it," Nick said, glancing over with a smile. "So, how's your snack?"

When Leo got into Nick's truck, there was a glossy white box with the Ginger's Breads logo on it waiting on the dashboard. Leo had been snacking on the treats since.

"Um, amazing," Leo said, glancing down at the savory mini quiche, scones, and cheesecakes. "But it's *Joel.* Does he do anything that isn't incredible?"

"Not that I've found."

"You want any? There's no way I can eat all this."

"Uhh, maybe? It'll be tough to do while I'm driving but sure."

"Good thing they're bite-sized," Leo said cheerfully. "So when did Joel start doing little boxes like this, anyway? I don't think I've ever seen them before."

"They might have been a special request," Nick said, sounding sheepish.

Leo gaped. "You had him make them for me?"

"Well, I mean, he does catering for the holidays and these are recipes he's already developed," Nick said. "So I can't take much credit. I just asked him to pack them up in a cute little box we could take with us."

"Still …" Leo smiled down at them. "They're great. So what do you want? Rosemary and ham quiche? Everything scone filled with salmon cream cheese? Tomato basil cheesecake? Beef, mushroom, and cranberry hand pie?"

"Yes," Nick said.

Laughing, Leo reached for one of the tiny quiches. "One of everything. Got it."

Although Leo didn't do anything but place the first of the delicious savory bites in Nick's outstretched hand, it kindled something warm in his chest.

He had no idea where they were going or what they were doing today, but he was in Nick's truck, listening to Christmas carols and sharing a special little meal with him.

Despite the embarrassing but sweet rescue, they were off to a good start.

CHAPTER FOURTEEN

"Oh my God," Leo said a short while later, his eyes widening as Nick turned into the driveway where a sign proudly displayed the Reindeer Rides Farm logo. Holy shit. "Are we … are we doing something with reindeer today?"

Nick shot him a grin. "Yes. I was trying to think of what you liked the most and it seems like you're a big fan of animals so … I thought the reindeer might be fun."

"Holy shit," Leo whispered. "That's … yes. Yes. Reindeer. Yes. I am *so* excited."

Nick shot him another grin, his eyes creasing at the corners. "Perfect."

Leo glanced around raptly as Nick parked by the barn and they got out of the truck. A man appeared, greeting Nick by name. Nick introduced him to Leo.

"So, you're here for a private reindeer experience," Ollie said when the intros were done.

"Um, I guess?" Leo shrugged, glancing over at Nick.

"Yep. You'll get to meet the reindeer, pet them, groom them, feed them …"

"This is the best day of my life," Leo said with a sigh. Holy shit, this was gonna be awesome. He couldn't wait to send photos to his family.

Nick beamed. "Are you ready?"

"So ready."

The barn was big and old, but very well maintained. The moment Leo stepped inside, he breathed in the familiar dusty scent of hay and straw and animals, feeling nostalgic for home.

The reindeer stared at them curiously as they approached the gate sectioning off a third of the barn. At the far end, big double doors were open to the pasture beyond.

Ollie gave them a few rules, then explained. "We don't usually do this. This is our first private reindeer experience so although they're used to humans, they might be skittish. Nick said you're familiar with animals though, Leo?"

"Oh yeah." Leo grinned. "My family has a dairy farm."

"Ahh." Ollie looked relieved. "Then you understand."

Leo nodded. He might not know reindeer but any large herd animal could be flighty and skittish with strangers, which could be dangerous.

Nick, who Leo knew didn't have any experience with anything larger than a cat or a dog, hung back, offering to take some pictures.

Ollie offered Leo a pail of their specialized feed. "You can put some in your hand and offer it to them, if you want."

Leo definitely wanted. He held out a hand and several of the animals eyed it curiously. One finally grew bold enough to step forward, reaching out with its nose to sniff his hand. With another wary look, it gobbled a few bites, then stepped back.

That went on for a few moments until Leo had a few of the reindeer nosing each other out of the way to eat from his hand.

He laughed, delighted. He glanced over to see Nick's soft expression. Warmth bloomed in Leo's chest.

It was so sweet of him to arrange this.

The reindeer were *amazing*. They were smaller than Leo anticipated. Half the size of a fully grown Jersey cow and they weighed about a third as much. And they were even cuter than he'd thought they'd be.

When the food was gone, Ollie held out a brush. "You can groom them, if you'd like."

"Oh, I'd like," Leo said happily. He carefully approached the friendliest of the reindeer, holding up the brush to show it what he was doing. He settled a hand on its flank, then carefully stroked the brush across its thick, shaggy fur.

It let out a soft huffing sound and leaned into him. Leo smiled.

"Would you like to know some facts about reindeer?" Ollie asked.

"Yes!" Leo said, giggling as another reindeer in front of him nosed at his pocket, hoping for more pellets.

"Well, unlike most deer, the female reindeer have antlers as well as the males," Ollie said.

"Huh." Leo scratched the nose of the one he was grooming. "So is this a lady reindeer or a gentleman?"

Ollie grinned. "This is a lady. We call her Gumdrop."

"Hi, Gumdrop," Leo whispered.

"They can't fly, but did you know they can swim?"

"No, I had no idea," Leo said, impressed.

"They have thick, wooly undercoats and the top layer of their fur is long and hollow shafted. It keeps them warm and increases buoyancy in the water."

"Very cool." Leo glanced over at Nick and smiled.

Nick beamed back again. Gah, he was such a sweetheart.

"They are also the only mammal who can see ultraviolet light," Ollie continued.

"Neat."

"And they have some of the richest and most nutritious milk of any land mammal."

"So, my family raises Jersey cows," Leo said, his interest piqued. "What's the butterfat percentage compared to that?"

Ollie grinned. "Twenty-two percent."

"Twenty-two?" Leo yelped. "Holy shit."

"Right? And ten percent protein."

"That's incredible."

Nick looked lost so Leo explained. "So, most milk is around three to five percent fat and like, three-and-a-half percent protein. Jersey milk is on the high end of that range for butterfat and a little higher in protein. About three point eight."

"You know your dairy," Ollie said admiringly.

"I do," Leo admitted. "Hazards of growing up on a dairy farm in Wisconsin."

"We have some milk and cheese right now," Ollie said. "Reindeer generally give birth in late spring or early summer and the calves are weaned in November and December. We don't milk them a lot. Frankly, they're very low yield. You can only get about one and a half to two cups per milking. But I could give you a taste if you're curious."

"*So* curious," Leo said with a laugh. "If you don't mind …"

"Not at all."

"So you're having fun?" Nick asked when Ollie left the barn.

"Oh my God, *so* much fun," Leo admitted, scratching under the reindeer's chin. "This is awesome. I miss animals more than I realized, I guess."

"Glad you're enjoying it."

"Do you want to pet one?" Leo asked. "I'll be nice and share Gumdrop with you."

"Sure." Nick stepped closer, reaching out a hand and letting the animal sniff before he carefully stroked her face. "Oh. Her coat is coarser than I expected."

"Yeah, it's not like a cat's fur. But it's very thick and warm."

"Yeah, it is." Nick slid a hand along Gumdrop's back and she leaned into the touch.

Gah, Leo couldn't blame her. He'd kinda like Nick to be touching him that way too.

"I love their faces," Leo said with sigh. "The big dark eyes and sweet little square noses get me. I can only imagine how cute the babies are."

"You could come back when they're born," Ollie said, reentering the barn carrying a tray. "If you're interested in seeing them. No charge."

"Um, yes. I'd love that."

"So, both of you can help yourself to the milk, cheese, and crackers," Ollie said, setting the tray on a nearby straw bale. "And here are some wipes to clean your hands."

"Thanks!"

After cleaning up, Nick and Leo sampled the milk and the sweet cheese, which was mild and creamy. Honestly, it reminded Leo a lot of cream cheese, only richer.

"I like it," he said. "What do you think?"

"Uhh, not to insult Gumdrop or you, Ollie, but I think I'll stick to cow's milk," Nick said with a cute wrinkle of his nose.

Leo grinned. His family had a small herd of goats and sheep as well, so he'd pretty much tried every kind of milk out there.

"So, are you ready for your ride?" Ollie asked when they were done.

"Uhh, hell yes," Leo said, visions of racing across the snowy ground on the back of a reindeer dancing in his head.

He said goodbye to Gumdrop and a few of the other reindeer, then followed Ollie and Nick out of the barn. He was disappointed when they walked around the back and there was a sleigh with reindeer harnessed to it.

"Oh, I thought we were going to actually ride them."

Ollie grinned. "The Sami people of northern Norway, Sweden, Finland, and Russia do. But we use sleighs. And at the risk of ruining the illusion even more, our sleighs use wheels. We don't get enough snow here in Illinois to use the traditional style sleighs with runners."

"Still very cool," Leo assured Nick, who looked worried.

A few minutes later, when they were tucked into the sleigh with a warm blanket over their laps, Leo snuggled close to Nick.

"Cold?" he asked, putting an arm around Leo.

"No." Leo glanced over. "Wanted to be close."

Nick swallowed. "Yeah?"

"Yeah," Leo said, reaching out to take Nick's gloved hand. "Today has been great so far."

As the sleigh moved over the snow, the bells on the reindeers harnesses jingling, hope rose inside Nick.

Leo was tucked close, his cheeks already flushed pink from the cool wind. He seemed happy and content and Nick was deeply relieved. He didn't think one good date was going to solve anything but he'd hoped to show Leo he was paying attention to him. That he knew him well enough to pick out what he'd enjoy.

It would take time and patience to show Leo how sincere he was. That he was reliable and trustworthy and in it for the long haul.

But some good dates couldn't hurt. And so far, this one was off to a great start.

"Where are we going now?" Leo asked.

"You'll see," Nick told him.

Leo poked him in the ribs. "Why are you trying to be so mysterious?"

"Because it's more fun."

Leo grumbled. "For one of us."

But he didn't look upset so Nick pulled him closer.

"Thank you," Leo said softly, a few minutes later. "I loved meeting the reindeer."

"I thought you might." Nick had hoped so, anyway.

"Honestly, it makes me miss home."

"Are you going to visit the Fenner Farm for Christmas?" Nick asked.

"No. My parents are coming to visit me," Leo said. "I think they were worried about me when we talked last."

"Because some guy was a jerk to you?" Nick asked.

"Something like that."

"So I'm going to have to win them over too," Nick said. "Unless … will that be too soon to meet the family?"

"Well, I guess we'll have to see how the next few weeks go. But I'd like for you to meet each other."

"Okay," Nick agreed. He was nervous. He'd never had to impress the parents before. He'd known Nicole's family growing up, so they'd already had a good idea of what kind of guy he was when he and Nicole had started dating.

"I didn't go into details, by the way," Leo said. "Just said there was a guy I was hoping it might work out with but he wasn't ready."

"Ahh." Well that was something.

"Hayden however …" Leo laughed ruefully. "He might take a while to come around."

"Shit."

"Sorry."

"Hey, you have nothing to be sorry about," Nick assured him. "This was on me."

Leo squeezed his hand. For a few moments they were silent and Nick glanced around, taking in the snow-covered ground and the rapidly deepening twilight. There were little fairy lights strung on the reindeer and it would be magical looking once it got fully dark.

"So you have two brothers, right?" Nick asked.

"Yes." Leo shifted, snuggling even closer. "Adam and Jason."

"Are they coming to visit for Christmas?"

"No. They're staying in Wisconsin to take care of the farm."

"Ohh, sure," Nick said. "Makes sense. Cows don't milk themselves."

Leo chuckled. "There are some robotic milking machines where the cows can walk up to the machine and it takes care of the whole thing without people, but that's for much bigger, fancier dairies."

"You know a lot about it," Nick observed. "It was great to hear you talk to Ollie. You sounded so smart and competent."

Leo straightened, grinning. "You like that, huh?"

"Yes."

"Hmm, good to know. I will *definitely* keep that in mind for the future." Leo settled back against his side, resting his cheek on Nick's shoulder. "You only have the one sister, Heather, yeah?"

"Yes. I used to be close to Nicole's brother, Ford, but like I said, he kinda disappeared from my life."

"Yeah, I remember you telling me about your encounter at the bookstore. It's hard when you drift away from people."

"It is," Nick admitted.

"Do you—do you want kids someday? The way you talked about Charlie …"

"Oh." Nick let out a shaky laugh. He forgot Leo wouldn't know that about him. Nick had read all of Leo's wants and needs in a relationship when he filled out the forms for the matchmaking service but Leo had never seen his. "Um, I do want kids. Nicole and I were trying. We found out shortly before she died that I have a low sperm count so we were looking into our options."

"Oh, Nick." Leo kissed his shoulder.

"Sometimes I'm glad," Nick whispered, his voice growing thick. "That we hadn't already had a kid or she wasn't pregnant when she died. That would have been …"

Leo squeezed him tighter. "I can only imagine."

"But um, yeah, I want to be a dad at some point. I was planning to be a stay-at-home dad. I was unhappy with my career at the bank and Nicole's books were selling so well it made the most sense."

"I love that," Leo said. "I, um, this is really, really putting the cart before the horse, or well, the sleigh before the reindeer, maybe, but I love my work so I kinda—I hoped to find a guy who wouldn't expect me to be the one home with the kids."

"Yeah?" Nick asked, hope rising in him.

"I want to be an active parent," Leo said. "Just … not the primary, stay-at-home one, if that makes sense."

"It does. And that would work for me," Nick said. "I mean, I know it's early for us to discuss this but I also think the relationships that tend to fail are the ones where people aren't on the same page about marriage and kids."

"Makes sense."

"So I don't think it's bad to talk about it when you're getting to know someone."

"Oh!" Leo sat up straight. "Oh, Nick, look at the lights!"

Nick grinned. It was fully dark now and they'd arrived in one of the neighborhoods on the outskirts of Santa's Village—what Christmas Falls called the center of town. All of the homes in the area had a ton of lights on them.

"Welcome to the second part of the date," Nick explained. "A sleigh ride and tour of the Christmas lights."

Leo kissed his cheek. "It's so *beautiful.*"

"Glad you like it."

"I do." Leo settled close again, his hat brushing Nick's cheek. "Hey, how do you feel about *Christmas Vacation*?"

"The movie?" Nick asked, slightly confused. "It's a classic, why?"

"Just curious."

The date ended with Nick dropping Leo off at his door with a hug.

No matter how great the evening had been, Nick needed to take everything slow this time around. But he was feeling optimistic as he let himself into his house and greeted Jelly.

She mewed before he had even gotten his coat off and he lifted her into the air triumphantly, then kissed the top of her head. "I have good feelings about this," Nick told her.

She squirmed and, laughing, he set her down.

He'd gotten her fed and settled into bed when his phone rang. He frowned at Leo's name, picking up immediately. "Hey, did you forget something in my truck?" he asked.

"No," Leo said. "I thought we'd keep doing the post-date debriefs."

Nick chuckled, settling back against the headboard. "Well, how'd your date go today?"

"Perfect," Leo said with a sigh. "He saved me from the evil

bathroom door, brought me yummy snacks, took me to pet some reindeer, then arranged for a romantic sleigh ride."

"Yeah? Well, I have it on good authority he had a great time too."

CHAPTER FIFTEEN

"So, how was the wine tasting date?" Nick asked a few days later after they both got home from the event.

Leo smiled, settling into his bed. "I had a fantastic time."

He thought of Nick's smile over the rim of the wineglass, the way he listened intently when Leo said what he liked about each one. He liked the way he'd introduced him to some friends he'd run into, and talked about future dates. On the way home, they'd also talked about their family holiday traditions. Laughing and reminiscing about good memories from the past, discussing what they'd like to do in the future.

It was a thousand times better than the date with Andrew 'Twinkle Toes' Mulford. Though, this time, Leo wouldn't have minded a *tiiiny* bit of groping.

Nick said, "I'm sure your date would be glad to hear it. He had a wonderful time too."

Leo grinned. Maybe the post-date debriefs were a little silly but he enjoyed them and it sounded like Nick did too.

"He was a perfect gentleman," Leo added. "A little bit *too* much of one."

"Oh yeah?"

"I mean, a hug at the end of the night and a kiss on the cheek is great but …"

"Feeling impatient, huh?"

Leo sighed. "I know he's being respectful and showing me he's not rushing things this time. But like … I kinda want to rush things."

"He is also tempted to rush," Nick admitted. "But he's trying very hard to show you he values you for a lot more than sex."

"I know." Leo *felt* valued. And very horny. "But like, bringing tools to fix my bathroom door was incredibly hot!"

Nick chuckled, his voice warm and low in Leo's ear. "Yeah?"

"I mean, I guess I have a competence kink too," Leo said. "But a man fixing stuff with his hands is always sexy."

Nick had cleared it with Joel of course, who had sounded both grateful for the help and miffed Leo hadn't mentioned the problem to him.

Secretly, Leo was glad it had been Nick to the rescue though. He'd been dressed casually in jeans and a flannel and Leo had watched avidly as he took the door off its hinges and used a small hand tool to shave the top of the door down. When he re-hung it, it worked perfectly.

"And now I'm thinking about him throwing me around like he manhandled that door," Leo admitted with a sigh.

"He'll definitely keep that in mind."

"What about on our next date?" Leo suggested hopefully.

"Mmm, he was planning to invite you to go on a boat ride to the falls."

"*After* the boat ride?" Leo asked hopefully.

"He'll take it under advisement."

"Tease!" Leo shot back.

"No, if I was being a tease, I'd take a picture of me in bed right now," Nick said, dropping the pretense they were talking about anyone else.

"I mean, you could do that toooo," Leo said, sliding his hand down his stomach because fuck that sounded hot.

"But I won't, because it's late and we both need some sleep," he said.

"Gah, you're such a responsible adult," Leo teased.

"Well, one of us has to be!"

Grinning, Leo wiggled to get comfortable. "Night, Nick. I won't be thinking about you when I jerk off before bed or anything."

Nick groaned. "Goodnight, Leo."

Leo was driving Nick crazy. He got more flirtatious with every day and Nick was losing his damn mind. He deserved it, though he didn't think Leo was doing it to tease or punish him or anything.

Leo was being his usual flirty self and Nick had to remember he was in this for the long haul.

If he wanted a future with Leo, slow and steady was the way to go. He didn't ever want to risk hurting Leo the way he'd done the first time they had sex.

But oh, it was sweet torture as Nick drove them to the outskirts of Christmas Falls and Leo had his hand on Nick's thigh, squeezing every so often as he talked about his workday.

"But you're probably sick of hearing about Zoom meetings," Leo said with a laugh as he finished the latest story.

"Never!" Nick assured him. "Though I think I'd lose my mind if I had that many corporate meetings."

"The jury's still out on that one for me," Leo said grimly.

Nick chuckled.

"So, how about you? Any good matches lately?"

"Yes, actually. A very sweet older couple. They knew each other in high school but went their separate ways and lost touch. She was widowed, he's divorced, and they were each other's second date. The moment they both got home from the date they sent me messages saying they didn't want to match with anyone else."

"Aww, that's adorable!" Leo said. He squeezed Nick's thigh again and Nick would *swear* it was higher this time.

"It's the best part of my job," he admitted.

Thankfully, they arrived at their destination a few minutes later and Nick parked the truck. "So we're going on a boat ride, yeah?"

"Yes. A boat tour of the falls the town was named after."

"Oh, this'll be fun. I've been wanting to do this for ages," Leo said, his eyes sparkling in the dim light of the cab.

Nick smiled. "I'm glad."

Once they were out of the truck, Nick took Leo's hand. Leo smiled, swinging their arms as they walked toward the ticket booth. After Nick had confirmed he'd already pre-paid for their tour, they followed the signs and glowing lanterns to the lake where a pontoon boat waited.

"Oooh. It's so pretty!" Leo said as they boarded the boat, craning his neck to look at the strings of Christmas lights. "Have you ever done this before?"

"Yes. A long time ago." He hoped Leo wouldn't mind that he'd done it with Nicole and some friends of hers from out of town, but Leo only smiled brighter and tugged Nick toward empty seats at the front end of the boat.

Nick was spreading throw blankets over them both when Leo earnestly said, "I hope Nicole would be happy we're dating."

Nick froze, glancing over, surprised but touched by the comment. "She would," he said hoarsely as he pulled Leo closer. "She'd be delighted. Second-chance romance was her favorite trope to write."

Leo grinned, squeezing his hand.

The tour started a short while later and they both fell silent, listening to the tour guide talk about the falls and the history of the area as they pulled away from the dock.

The boat cruised slowly toward the low cliffs and everyone on board gasped when they got their first clear glimpse of the lit-up falls. There were no big mountains in this area but the water poured over a low cliff, flowing over two tiered outcroppings before finally landing on the lake's surface, creating a riot of foam.

Little prisms of water droplets glittered in the lights at the base of the falls and Leo let out another gasp, loud enough to hear over the roar of the falls. "It's so *beautiful*, Nick."

Nick smiled, kissing Leo's temple and feeling the soft wool of his hat tickling his lips. "I'm glad you like it."

"I *love* all of these dates you've planned. You're amazing," Leo said with sigh. "I hope you know that."

Nick squeezed Leo tighter.

They both took a few pictures of the falls and they were trying to manage a selfie with the falls in the background when a nearby woman asked if they'd like her help. They both enthusiastically agreed and she snapped a few shots of them.

They stared at Leo's phone after, heads bent together, as they looked at the photos. Nick had been worried they'd look too dark or blurry because of the lighting but they'd turned out great.

"We look so good together," Leo said.

"Are you surprised?" Nick asked, amused.

"A little bit," Leo admitted. "At first, I thought you were straight. And out of my league."

"Neither are true," Nick said fiercely, gently touching Leo's face until he could look him in the eye. "Maybe I felt that too when I first realized I was attracted to you. You're so *vibrant* and full of life and optimistic and I … I wondered if maybe you wouldn't want to be with someone so much older who'd been through all of this heavy stuff and—"

"Never," Leo said fiercely. "I'm sorry you had to go through it but I don't think it makes you any less *worthy* of love because you're grieving the fact you lost it. I know you're capable of deep love. That's the kind of guy I *want* to be with."

He kissed Leo then, a brief brush of their lips and a promise of more to come.

Leo blinked, clearly surprised, before he let out a happy sigh and burrowed close. The boat moved again, pulling away from the falls for the return trip to shore.

An hour later, as Nick pulled into the lot behind the bakery and parked, reluctant to see the night end. He wanted to lean in and kiss Leo. He wanted to let it grow so heated he let himself be dragged upstairs to Leo's bed.

"What are you thinking about?" Leo whispered, his voice hushed. "The way you're looking at me …"

"Thinking about how much I want you," Nick admitted. "How much I wish I could go upstairs with you."

"You're the only one stopping you." Leo's tone was laced with humor but it was true. Nick was the one doing this to himself.

"I know. But I—I want to woo you."

Leo bit his lip, grabbing the front of Nick's jacket. "But you don't have to keep wooing me, Nick. I'm already thoroughly wooed."

"Never," Nick said huskily. He reached up and brushed his thumb across Leo's cheek. "If we do keep seeing each other, I'll spend the rest of our lives wooing you."

"Ohh." Leo blinked. "Oh, Nick. Kiss me. *Please*."

Nick smiled as he leaned in, brushing his lips across Leo's cheek before he drew back.

Leo huffed. "Not what I meant."

"A little longer, please?" Nick murmured. "Be patient with me. It's important I take my time."

Leo searched his face for a long moment before he nodded and kissed Nick's cheek. "Yeah, of course."

CHAPTER SIXTEEN

"We're a total cliché gay couple," Leo said happily as they left The White Elephant. "We had brunch and we're going antiquing!"

Nick chuckled, "A couple, huh?" he asked.

Leo glanced over, suddenly doubting himself. "I mean … if you *want* to be."

"Yes," Nick said firmly, reaching out to take Leo's hand. "I want to."

"So does this mean we can have sex now?" Leo asked. "Because I'm willing to skip the antiquing for sex. That's pretty gay too."

Nick snorted. "You *need* a desk," he pointed out.

"Do I? Or do I need dick?" he mused.

Nick made a choking sound. "Leo!"

"What?" He gave Nick an innocent look. "I'm just saying …"

“You’re a menace.” Nick bumped his shoulder.

“You like that about me,” Leo said confidently.

Nick paused and Leo came to an abrupt stop, rocking back on his heels before Nick tugged and reeled him in before pressing him against the nearby brick wall. “Yeah, I do,” he said huskily. “I really do like you.”

Leo smiled happily. Nick was so … Gah, he looked *good* today. He always looked good of course but he seemed very light and very happy, handsome in his dark gray jeans, weathered brown boots, and green hoodie. He’d paired it with a knitted charcoal beanie and a black wool coat and he looked so cozy and stylish and …

“God, when you look at me like that …” Nick whispered.

“How do I look at you?” Leo asked.

“Like you’re starving.”

“I am.” Leo’s stomach was full of tasty eggnog French toast and turkey sage breakfast sausage but it wasn’t that kind of hunger.

“Desk,” Nick said, like he was trying to remind himself.

“Dick,” Leo countered.

“*Desk*,” Nick repeated, pressing his forehead to Leo’s for a second. “You were complaining the other day that your back hurt.”

Honestly, Leo had hoped Nick would touch him more but that had totally backfired when Nick gifted him with an appointment for a massage. Which would be lovely but not what he had in mind.

"Desk *then* dick?" Leo tried, though he wasn't *actually* trying to rush Nick. He understood why Nick needed to take it slow. But the teasing banter was fun.

"Desk today, dick soon."

Leo batted his lashes. "Soon is like … today, maybe?"

"This week," Nick countered.

Leo blinked, surprised. He'd been prepared to wait a lot longer. "Really?"

"Yeah. I have one more date planned. And I was thinking after, if we both wanted it …"

"I do," Leo said eagerly.

Nick smiled and Leo suddenly noticed how long his lashes were. *Gah.* He was so handsome.

"Then we're in agreement."

"Shake on it?" Leo said.

Amused, Nick held out a hand. "Deal."

Happy to know the probably-necessary-but-seriously-annoying ban on sex finally had an end date, Leo tugged Nick toward the antique shop. "Come on! What are you waiting for? I need a desk!"

Laughing, Nick fell into step beside him.

Nick let Leo lead as they browsed the Merry Memories antique shop. He waved at the owner, Liam Barlowe, who gave him a vague wave back before returning his attention to his laptop screen.

Nick had been here dozens of times and he always loved the mix of expensive pieces and semi-trashy junk cluttering the place. He liked poking around for treasures and gently poking fun at terrible, ugly things. He hoped Leo would like it too.

The first time Leo turned, holding out a weird, gaudy object and breathily said, "What is this? It's *hideous* and I love it," Nick felt it square in his chest, like an unexpected snowball to the sternum.

Oh. *Oh*, he knew this feeling. He was falling in love.

Dazed, he followed in Leo's wake, listening to him chatter on about the merits of possible desks for his apartment and a painting of a forlorn-looking cow he wanted to take home and hang in his living room.

He tried on goofy oversized red sunglasses and a Santa hat, begging Nick to get a picture of him wearing them.

Nick must have seemed normal to Leo but all he could think about was the word *love*, echoing over and over like a heartbeat, pulsing in his ears and filling his body all the way to his toes.

In the end, Leo bought a handful of items, including the sad cow portrait, but no desk.

"I don't know," he said with a sigh as he got into Nick's truck. "Like, the oak table is cool but I need more storage. And I love the desk with the pretty veneer drawer fronts but, honestly, it needed some work, you know? It feels like a lot to pay for something that could stand to have the feet repaired and the whole thing refinished. I wouldn't mind doing it myself if I had a place to work on it but I don't and, I dunno, it doesn't feel very *practical*."

"True," Nick agreed, already planning to come back and get the desk tomorrow. He should call the owner, Liam, today so no one stole it out from under him … Did he have time to refinish it for Leo before Christmas? Worst-case scenario, he'd give him an IOU on the desk for Christmas but he'd like to present it to him all finished if he could.

"Have you done a lot of furniture restoration?" Nick asked, curious.

Leo shrugged. "Not a ton since I lived at home but I used to help my dad with projects. And sometimes when I was living in Chicago, I'd find something sturdy but ugly left on the curb and take it back to my apartment and paint it."

"Cool. Those are handy skills to have." Something else he and Leo had in common.

"Yeah. They can be fun projects."

They arrived at the bakery a short while later. Nick parked and Leo immediately turned to him. "So, do you want to come up for a bit?"

Nick raised an eyebrow.

"Not for sex," Leo said hastily. "Despite all of my teasing earlier, I can totally be patient, especially now I know there's an end in sight. I thought … I dunno. Maybe you're sick of me already but I kinda don't want today to end."

"How could I be sick of you?" Nick asked, confused.

Leo shrugged. "Sometimes people say I'm a lot."

"You're wonderful," Nick said honestly. "And yeah, I'd love to come up. What did you have in mind?"

"Having a lazy evening," Leo said. "Nothing special. We could watch a movie—oh, or there's a hockey game on tonight. I thought we'd eat dinner and just … you know, chill. I love all of the dates and going out and doing stuff. But I thought some quiet time together would be good too."

"Yeah," Nick said, surprised but pleased by the idea. "That sounds perfect."

He parked and helped Leo carry his purchases up to his apartment.

"So, I'm not hungry-hungry," Leo said after they'd hung the cow portrait and washed a couple of colorful vintage mugs and bowls. "But I will be in like an hour or so. How do you feel about Bratwurst Hot Dish?"

"I know what bratwurst is, but what's hot dish?"

"Oh." Leo laughed. "Upper Midwest thing. The short answer is that it's a casserole."

"Oh, sure," Nick said. "I like brats and casserole. Never had them together but …"

Leo grinned, shrugging out of his cardigan and rolling up his sleeves to wash his hands. "So this recipe is my grandma's and it's like … peak German-immigrant-turned-dairy-farmer-in-Wisconsin vibes."

"I'm intrigued." Nick leaned against the counter. "Tell me more."

"So, we start by boiling some brats in chicken broth."

"Want some help?" Nick asked, pushing up his sleeves too.

"Sure, sounds great."

Leo prepped stuff while Nick took care of the boiling. After the brats were cooked and cut up into little slices, Nick watched Leo brown them in butter.

"Oh shit," Leo said as he pulled out a can of sauerkraut. "Um, do you like this stuff? Not everyone does."

"I don't eat it a lot," Nick said with a shrug. "But my mom used to do pork chops with sauerkraut and apples every fall and winter when Heather and I were growing up and I liked that."

"Cool." Leo grinned. "Sounds yummy. You can make it for me sometime."

Nick grinned back, watching Leo layer the drained sauerkraut and bratwurst. He whisked together cream of cheddar soup and milk, poured that over everything else, then layered frozen tater tots on top.

Leo put it into the oven with a flourish, then said, "Now, let's go make out on the couch."

"I thought you were going to behave," Nick teased, but he followed Leo into the living room anyway.

"Just making out, I swear," Leo said, holding up his hands, palms facing out. "I'll be so good."

Nick was impressed Leo thought *he* had that kind of willpower but he settled on the couch, stretched out on his back and crooked a finger. "Come here."

Leo let out a happy sigh and settled into position, lying half on top of Nick. Nick brushed his thumb across Leo's cheek, then kissed him softly, nipping at Leo's lower lip before he drew back. "Did you set a timer?" he asked. "Because I can already tell I'm going to lose track of time."

"Oh shit." Leo wriggled to get his phone out of his pocket. "Good call."

After the alarm was set, he tossed his phone onto the coffee table. Smiling, he settled into Nick's arms again. "Now, where were we?"

"Right about here," Nick said, pulling him even closer.

To his surprise, Leo was slow and deliberate. He kept his hands on Nick's chest or in his hair and he kissed Nick like he wasn't trying to rush anything. Nick was hard when Leo pulled away, flushed and panting. And he watched greedily as Leo adjusted his dick in his jeans.

"Fuck," he said, without meaning to and Leo gave him a molten look.

"Am I going to have to tell *you* to behave?"

"Probably," Nick admitted.

"Well, it's nice to feel wanted," Leo said.

Nick blinked. "Oh, Leo, I want you. I want you so much I can hardly think straight sometimes."

He leaned in for another kiss and Leo let out a low sound, wiggling closer. Nick tilted his head, deepening the kiss, letting his tongue slip between Leo's lips. Nick gasped at the feel of Leo's hand sliding under his shirt, his palm warm against his skin.

"This okay?" Leo murmured, touching his lips to the corner of Nick's mouth.

"Yeah. Yeah, it's good. Kiss me."

They kissed again and again, until Nick was dizzy with it and he could feel his cock pressing against his fly. Leo was rubbing up against his hip, his thigh slotted between Nick's, hard and eager.

"Fuck, you feel so good," Nick rasped. He reached down, getting a handful of Leo's ass and squeezing.

"Oh, God, we should stop," Leo said, burying his face against Nick's throat, his breathing coming in short, warm puffs of air.

"I know."

But Leo grazed his teeth along Nick's Adam's apple, making Nick shudder. Leo's hips moved in soft rolling waves, his ass clenching and relaxing under Nick's grip.

Nick did nothing to stop him.

"God, Nick, I'm getting close." Leo whimpered after a while, clutching at his upper arm.

"You can come, if you want," Nick murmured. "I'm going to keep it in my pants but if you think you can come like this, I want to make you feel good."

"Fuck, really?"

"Yeah." Nick felt a sudden urgency to give Leo this orgasm now, to make him feel good and take nothing in return. "Yeah, I want to see you let loose."

"Oh God." Leo panted, rocking his hips harder and faster against Nick's thigh, breath growing ragged. Flushed from the heat of their bodies, Nick got a better grip on Leo's ass and helped him move, coaxing him into a quick, fluid rhythm. "Fuck," he whimpered.

"Let go, Leo," Nick murmured. "Let me feel you come."

With a short, sharp cry, Leo went still, sinking his teeth into the fabric below Nick's collarbone. His hips shuddered, his entire body trembling as he rode out the orgasm in Nick's arms.

It seemed to go on and on, so Nick held Leo, stroking his hair and letting him come down from it while he murmured how amazing he was. How good he felt in Nick's arms.

When Leo finally lifted his head, his expression was dazed and overwhelmed. His cheeks were pink and his hair damp along his hairline. "Nick," he said breathlessly. "That was …"

Nick smiled, brushing his thumb across Leo's cheek, utterly charmed by him. "Good, I hope."

"So good." He bit his lip, finally letting go of the death grip he'd had on Nick's arm. He slid his hand lower, hesitating at Nick's waist. "Do you want me to …"

"No." Nick pressed a kiss to Leo's forehead, tasting the faint traces of salt from his sweat. "That was all for you."

"You're so hard though."

"Yeah," Nick admitted ruefully. "I am. But that's okay. It won't kill me."

"You're so *nice*," Leo said affectionately.

"You deserve nice," Nick told him. "You deserve nice things and nice people in your life."

Leo gave him a smile, propping his head on his fist to look at him. His forearm dug into Nick's ribs and Nick's lower leg was going numb but he didn't want to move. Didn't want to do anything to break the moment.

But as he was about to say that, Leo's phone let out a jazzy little chime. Leo grumbled, mashing his face into Nick's chest. "Damn it."

He levered himself off the couch, turned off the alarm, then glanced down at Nick with a rueful smile. "I guess I do need to get cleaned up."

There was a damp spot on his jeans near the fly and Nick resisted the urge to reach out and brush his fingers across the denim.

"I'd offer to help but …" Nick said with a groan as he sat up, swinging his legs around to settle his feet on the floor.

"Yeah, we'd be breaking our rules." Leo sighed.

Honestly, maybe they already had but Nick felt good about the flushed, happy look on Leo's face. He could never regret that.

Nick stood, gently grasping Leo's hip and leaning forward for a kiss. "Go get cleaned up," he murmured. "I'll take care of dinner."

"Okay." Leo shot him a smile. "Thanks, Nick."

He wasn't entirely sure what Leo was thanking him for. The orgasm? The help with dinner? But he merely nodded and gently swatted Leo's ass. "Go!"

Leo's smile turned into a grin but he walked toward the hall. "Oh! Don't forget to put the grated cheese on, then put the hot dish in for another ten or fifteen minutes, please," he called out.

"Will do," Nick said, smiling after him. Having something to focus on would distract him from the hard-on he had.

Maybe.

"So how is it?" Leo asked. He'd mopped up, then changed into fresh underwear and pajama pants and they were now eating hot dish on the couch out of Leo's new bowls, watching the Evanston River Otters play the Dallas Steers.

Evanston wasn't winning. Shocker. Though Gabriel Theriault had made a *beauuutiful* goal earlier.

Nick glanced up. "The hot dish? It's good. I like it."

"Yeah? You're not just saying that to be nice?"

"No. Why would I do that?"

"I dunno."

"Hey," Nick said, bumping Leo's knee with his. "I wouldn't lie to you. Or even stretch the truth. If it was only okay, I'd tell you I appreciated you making it but it wasn't my favorite. And if I hated it, I'd tell you it wasn't for me. But I always try to say what I mean."

"Good." Leo smiled down at his nearly empty bowl. "Want seconds?"

"Half scoop?" Nick asked, holding his own bowl out.

"I can do that." Still smiling, Leo carried the bowls into the kitchen. He snapped a few shots of the partially decimated hot dish to send to his family.

From the living room, Nick let out a whoop. "Hey! Joel's cousin scored a goal!"

"Jamie Walsh?" Leo called back as he refilled the bowls.

"Yeah!"

Leo returned to the living room in time to catch the replay. "Ooh, that's a nice one too."

"Right?"

"Now they're only down by three," Leo said, laughing.

"Yeah, they're not having the best season, huh?" Nick said with a wry grin as he dug into his bowl.

"Not so much. Fun to watch though."

"Totally."

The hot dish was still steaming, so Leo set his bowl down and pulled out his phone.

He edited a few photos from their day together, then attached them to the family group chat and typed out a message. He hesitated before he hit *Send*.

"Hey, you're okay with me sending some pictures of our dates and stuff to my family and telling them you're my boyfriend, right?"

Nick glanced over, fork frozen midway to his mouth. "Of course. I mean, I'm fine with partner too if you prefer."

Leo smiled. That wasn't what he'd meant. He'd been asking about Nick being okay with making it official to his family but that definitely answered that question.

"I'll post on social media too," he said after he hit *Send*, feeling daring.

Nick smiled. "Oh, that reminds me. We should follow each other. I was going to tag you in some stuff I posted the other day but I realized I didn't have your username. Hope that was okay I posted it. I should have asked first but …"

"Sure," Leo said, surprised. "I mean, yeah, we should follow each other and of course it's okay."

He put down his phone in favor of eating, but he was halfway through his bowl before a thought occurred to him. "Did you *come out* on social media, Nick?"

"Yeah, inadvertently." He huffed out a laugh. "I didn't even think about it. I've known I was bi for so long it never occurred to me that there would be much of a reaction to it but apparently, I surprised a lot of people who didn't know."

"Did you run into any issues?"

"Oh, a few." Nick shrugged. "I always figure it's the trash taking itself out though. Saves me the trouble of having to block them if they unfollow me."

"You're very … chill about this," Leo said.

Nick gave him a crooked smile. "My sister's a lesbian. I've been working with LGBTQ+ clients for years. Yeah, it's new to *me* but it's not like all of this came as a big shock. Did you expect me to have a big sexuality crisis about dating a man?"

"No!" Leo protested. "And I don't want you to. I just expected you to be a bit … hesitant about being public about it or something. Cause people can be shitty sometimes."

Nick frowned. "They can. But, Leo, I'm all in on this relationship. I'm excited about our future and I want people to know I'm happy. That there's hope after loss."

Tears welled up and Leo set down his bowl and scooted closer. "Oh, Nick," he whispered.

“Hey, what is it?” Nick said, wiping away a tear. “What’s wrong?”

“I’m so happy,” he said, although that word didn’t come close to covering everything he felt.

“I am too.” Nick pulled him closer, whispering in his ear. “For the first time in years, I’m really happy and excited about the future again. And that’s because of you, Leo.”

CHAPTER SEVENTEEN

Leo was in a fantastic mood as he crunched through the snow on the way to Nick's house on Tuesday night.

Christmas Eve was in a week and Leo was done with work until after the holiday. He had a hot boyfriend, his family was eager to meet said hot boyfriend when they came to visit soon, and tonight, he and Nick were *definitely* having sex.

He patted the messenger bag slung over his shoulder. It contained his toothbrush, condoms, and other overnight supplies.

He whistled as he walked down the sidewalk, cheerfully greeting familiar faces.

"Oooh, I like your lights!" he exclaimed as he passed one house, where a mom and kids were getting out of their SUV. "They're so pretty!"

"Thanks, Leo!" Stephanie called back.

He practically skipped the rest of the block to Nick's house. It glowed with lights too and when Nick opened the door,

Leo said, "Hi! Your place looks amazing. The lights make it look like a gingerbread house!"

"Hi. Thank you." Nick leaned in and kissed his cheek. "You look great too. Come in."

"Thanks!" Leo stepped inside and sniffed the air. "Ooh, something smells fantastic."

"Well," Nick said, settling a hand low on Leo's back. "I hope this wasn't too presumptuous of me but it's baked spaghetti. Your *mom's* baked spaghetti."

"You contacted my mom?" Leo asked, flabbergasted as Nick helped him off with his bag and coat. How? Maybe Nick had used the contact form on the dairy's website? But if he had, it would have gone to one of Leo's brothers, who would totally have teased Leo for it. His mom never checked the company's email. Hell, she barely checked her own email.

"No. But Hayden had the recipe."

"Oh. *Clever.*"

"I asked him what you'd like for dinner and he suggested it," Nick admitted. "We had a good long talk. He was pretty wary about me, given the way I bailed on you there, but I think he understands now what happened and why I messed up. It was about more than just getting the recipe, you know?"

Leo kissed his cheek again, touched that Nick wanted to make sure his friend understood. "Well, that was thoughtful of you to reach out to him."

"That's my middle name."

Leo grinned, kicking off his boots and lining them up on the tray to drip dry. "Nicholas Thoughtful Morgan. That has a ring to it."

Nick laughed. "It's Theodore, so same initials."

Leo made a face. "My name is ridiculous."

"Yeah?"

"Leopold Hausch Fenner. If you can't tell, the first two come from my mom's side. Her father was German and she named me after him."

"Ahh. There are a lot of Germans in Wisconsin, aren't there?"

"Yes. Hence the hot dish we made the other night."

"Well, you'll have to settle for the baked spaghetti tonight."

"I can handle that." Leo smiled, touched by the gesture. Besides, maybe this was his Upper Midwest talking, but how could anyone not love a cozy casserole in the winter?

Comfort food was the bomb.

"Want the five-cent tour of the place?" Nick asked, holding out a hand.

"Sure!" All he'd ever seen before was the office and he'd entered through the back door.

Hand-in-hand Nick gave Leo a tour around the modest but beautiful bungalow. There were original wood floors and trim throughout. It looked like the kitchen had been updated recently but the soft, buttery-yellow cabinets and retro-style appliances made it blend seamlessly into the old home.

"These are the stairs down to the basement," Nick said when they were back in the hallway, opening the door halfway, then abruptly shutting it. "But it's not that exciting. Just an unfinished space with laundry and utility stuff. Not worth seeing. Lots of spiders."

Leo shrugged, letting Nick drag him down the hall to a small guest room he used as a home gym. Leo smiled when they passed through the dining room and spotted the table laid out for two with flowers and candles.

"Romantic," he commented and Nick smiled too.

"This is my bedroom," Nick said, when they were upstairs, standing in the doorway. "I, uh, repainted it this summer and got a new bed. A … refresh for my life, I guess. I didn't do it thinking about bringing a new partner in but …" He shrugged, smiling at Leo bashfully. "Now I'm glad I did."

"It's beautiful," Leo assured him, pressing their shoulders together.

Curled up in the middle of the bed was a cat. "Ohh, is that Jelly?" he asked, delighted to finally meet her.

Her ear flicked, like she'd heard her name, but she snoozed on.

"Yep." Nick let go of his hand. "You can pet her."

"Nah, I'll let her sleep," Leo said. "I'm sure we'll have plenty more opportunities to meet."

Nick leaned in, pressing a kiss to Leo's lips. It was soft and gentle, the type of kiss that was merely a sweet touch, not a prelude to anything else. There would be plenty of time for that later too.

They returned to the first floor and Nick grabbed a bottle of red wine from the built-in wooden sideboard and held it out. "Would you like some with dinner?"

"Sure!" Leo inspected the bottle. "Hey, this red blend is from the wine tasting. Good memory. Uh, yours for remembering the wine I mentioned I liked best, that is. Not my memory of that awful date with Twinkle Toes."

Nick snorted and handed him a wine key. "Did I tell you I let Andrew go as a client?"

"Nooo," Leo said, peeling away the foil on the bottle. "Why?"

"Because I gave him a warning after his date with you. I told him if behaved that way again and touched anyone who didn't want it, he'd be out on his ass."

Leo wrinkled his nose. "And he did it again?"

Nick sighed. "He did."

"Gross." Leo twisted the wine key into the cork.

"Yeah, some guys never learn."

"Nick?" Leo said, the cork popping as he pulled it free of the bottle. "Did you deliberately set me up with bad dates?"

Nick sighed, leaning against the nearby wall. "I don't know. I mean, consciously? Absolutely not. Without realizing it? Maybe? Clearly it was a conflict of interest for me. I've absolutely *never* dated a client or even wanted to before."

"Until me," Leo said happily. That made him feel very special.

"Until you." Nick stepped forward, brushing his lips across Leo's. "Now, I'm going to get dinner on the table. It should be ready to come out of the oven any minute."

"Need help with anything?" Leo asked.

"You could pour the wine and light the candles. There are matches in the drawer there." He pointed to the sideboard.

"I can do that!"

A short while later, they sat down to enjoy their dinner.

It turned out, there was more than spaghetti and red wine for dinner. There was a salad and a chai spice streusel-topped apple pie too.

"From Ginger's Breads," Nick explained as he brought out the plates with little dollops of vanilla ice cream melting on top. "I wasn't going to try to compete with Joel on pie baking. I know I'd lose."

"I *am* in love with his baked goods," Leo admitted.

Nick shot him a look. "As long as it's just his baked goods."

Leo shrugged, licking off his fork. "Well, he has a pretty nice ass …"

Nick's look of outrage made Leo giggle. "Excuse me. I think mine is every bit as good," he sputtered.

"Well, I guess I'll have to do a long, *thorough* examination later," he teased.

"Of my ass, or Joel's?" Nick scowled.

Leo snorted. "*Yours* of course."

"Better be."

By the end of dessert, Leo was pleasantly full, relaxed from the wine, and totally falling in love with the guy who'd made it all happen.

"This was perfect," Leo said, sighing a little dreamily.

"Everything. Including the pie. How'd you know apple was my favorite?"

Nick shrugged. "Hayden helped there too."

"Now, I'm not complaining about the ice cream," Leo said. "But some time I want to introduce you to the way my family eats pie."

"Yeah?"

"Yeah. We do a few slices of cheddar with it. On top, if the pie is still warm so it melts. My grandpa *loved* that."

"Any excuse for cheese, huh?"

"Pretty much," Leo agreed, smiling. You could take the guy out of Wisconsin but you couldn't take the cheese out of him. Or something.

"I'd love to try cheddar on apple pie sometime." Nick's eyes glowed warmly in the candlelight.

Leo tried not to swoon. This man was … everything good in the world.

Leo got up and coaxed Nick to scoot back so he could sit on his lap. "I teased earlier but I hope you know *you're* the one I want to be with," he said huskily. "No one else."

Nick smiled. "That goes both ways." He patted Leo's hip. "But we should get up. These chairs are vintage and I'm not sure how much weight they can hold."

"I did eat a lot of spaghetti," Leo agreed, standing. "They might be in real danger."

Nick chuckled, stacking the plates. Leo helped, and in no time, the table was clear.

"So." Nick said, after they'd filled the dishwasher and tidied the kitchen. "How would you feel about a Christmas movie in front of the fire?"

"Yes please." Come to think of it, Nick *hadn't* shown him the living room yet.

When they stepped inside, Leo understood why. There was already a nest of cushy pillows and blankets on the floor and the Christmas tree glowed with lights.

"Get comfy," Nick said. "I'll light the fire."

Leo took a seat, burrowing into the fluffy pile. "Oh my God, Nick, this is *heaven*."

Smiling, Nick crouched in front of the brick fireplace and a moment later, the fire glowed as brightly as the tree. Nick lit a few candles around the room as well, then smiled down at Leo, flipping off the overhead light. "Be right back."

"I'll be here!" Leo promised. He pulled out his phone and took a few pictures of the fire and tree. He made sure his phone was on silent, then tossed it onto the couch so it wouldn't interrupt anything.

A few moments later he heard a chirp and glanced over to see Jelly trotting toward him. "Oh, hi, sweetheart," he crooned. "I'm Leo."

The cat sniffed his hand, then butted against it, demanding pets. Leo laughed delightedly. "Oh aren't you a friendly one?" he said, smiling. "I think I love you already."

He dropped his voice. "And I am totally falling for your human. He is …"

Leo sighed, resting his cheek on a pillow as he petted the cat, still feeling the dreamy contentment from earlier. Nick had made the evening so perfect already. And the night had only begun.

"Well, don't you both look cozy?" Nick said with a smile a few minutes later as he stepped into the living room. "Hope there's some room for me."

"Always," Leo said, sitting up and patting the spot by his hip. Jelly made a disgruntled noise.

"Boozy peppermint hot chocolate and whipped cream," Nick said, handing over a mug. "I have it on good authority you prefer whipped cream to marshmallows."

Touched, Leo stared at the mug. "Oh, Nick. God, you thought of *everything*."

"Well, I figured I'd let you pick out what movie you want to watch." Nick shrugged, taking a seat beside him.

Leo kissed his cheek. "*The Holiday*, obviously. It's really old. I think it came out when I was like … in first or second grade or something, but it's *peak* Christmas romance. You can't go wrong with Nancy Meyers directing."

"*Old*." Nick reached for a remote. "It came out when I was twenty. That makes *me* feel old."

Leo chuckled. He didn't think a lot about Nick being thirteen years older than him but he supposed this *did* highlight that. But as long as they could laugh about it, what did it matter?

"I like that you're a bit older than me," Leo admitted, taking a sip of the hot chocolate. "I think that was part of my problem finding someone who was looking for the same thing I was. The guys my age wanted to fuck around. They didn't really get *romance*. Not the way I wanted, anyway. Not the way you show it."

"Good." Nick navigated to the movie and pressed *Play*. "Their loss is my gain."

Smiling, Leo took another sip of cocoa and tipped his head to the side, resting it on Nick's soft, burgundy sweater-covered shoulder. Yeah, he was done for.

He'd finally found the man of his dreams.

They talked about their favorite scenes and Leo glowed, enjoying that Nick seemed to revel in the small moments the way Leo did. He'd dated a guy for a while who hated talking during movies at all and refused to discuss it after.

Like, where was the fun in that?

But when it came to the part where Jude Law's character, Graham, revealed he'd been widowed, Leo froze, scrambling for the remote to pause the movie. "Oh, shit, I forgot about that part. Are you sure you want to watch this?" he asked, glancing at Nick.

Nick gave him a soft smile. "Yeah. I appreciate you worrying about it but honestly, I feel like I'm in a great place right now."

"Okay, good," Leo said. "But you'll tell me if that changes?"

"I'll tell you," Nick promised. He leaned over and pressed his lips to Leo's cheek. "And thank you. I appreciate how thoughtful you are. And, you know what? It turns out I like nice guys too."

Leo gave him a smile and hit *Play* again.

After Nick and Leo finished their hot cocoa, Nick threw a few more logs on the fire. They curled up together in the nest of pillows, resuming their commentary on their favorite parts of the movie as it played out in front of them.

When the movie was over, Leo sighed happily, feeling drowsy and content in Nick's arms. "That was *great*."

"It was." Spooned around him now, Nick kissed the back of his neck. "I guess sometimes going to a new place is the best way to find love."

"Worked for me," Leo said without thinking.

Nick drew in a sharp breath. "Leo?" he rose on one elbow.

"Oh shit," Leo whispered, worried he'd gone too fast. "I …"

"Hey, look at me." Nick coaxed Leo to roll over to face him. He cupped Leo's cheek. "Do you mean it?"

"Yeah, I … I'm definitely falling in love with you." He hadn't *thought* about it that hard but what else could this be?

"Good," Nick said firmly. "Because I'm falling in love with you too. I realized it the other day at Merry Memories. You were having so much fun and *I* was having fun and it just hit me."

"Oh, Nick." Leo leaned in, softly kissing him.

He didn't know how to say everything he was feeling at the moment so he poured it into the kiss, letting it turn hotter and wetter. Deeper.

Nick responded, groaning against his mouth and he pulled Leo's body tighter against his. "Hey, do you want to take this upstairs?" Nick asked roughly, sliding a hand down Leo's side and gripping his hip.

Leo shook his head. "No, right here is perfect, if you want."

Nick bit at his neck. "I just want you."

"Oh God, I want you too, Nick."

Nick flipped him onto his back and Leo stared, biting his lip when Nick eased the zipper down on his jeans and worked them off. Nick brushed soft kisses against his thighs, alternating them with nips and licks until Leo let out a groan. "Fuck. Nick …"

He shifted forward, brushing his lips over Leo's cock, his breath warm, even through the stretchy fabric of Leo's underwear. He did it again, mouthing and kissing him, until Leo twisted under him, seeking more.

"I want these gone," Nick murmured, tugging at Leo's underwear, and he lifted his hips, allowing Nick to slide the fabric down his legs and off.

Nick took Leo's dick in his hand but for the first time, he looked apprehensive as he stroked lightly. "I've never done this," he said quietly. "Uh, sucked cock before."

"Hey, that's okay," Leo assured him, reaching out to touch his face. "You do whatever you feel comfortable with. I'm sure I'll like it."

"But I want you to enjoy it."

The stubborn note in Nick's voice made Leo smile. "You'll be touching me. It'll be perfect. And if it's something you like having done to you, chances are I'll enjoy it." He shrugged, because really, although he understood why Nick might need a moment to adjust, it didn't *have* to be complicated.

"Okay."

Leo stroked Nick's cheek again, then settled onto his back. "You can start with what you were doing to my thighs and over the fabric. That felt *amazing*."

Nodding, Nick shifted onto his elbows. Leo closed his eyes at the first brush of Nick's warm breath on his sensitive skin. He shivered at the sensation and a moment later he felt a soft peck, then a longer, broader lick.

At first, Nick *was* hesitant, halting sometimes like he was thinking hard about everything he did. When Leo let out a quiet moan, it seemed to ignite something in him. It wasn't long before Nick wrapped his hand around the base of Leo's cock and swiped his tongue across the head.

Leo gasped, reaching out to clutch Nick's shoulder. "Yeah. *That.* Keep going," he pleaded.

With a soft chuckle, Nick continued, growing bolder and more sure of himself. He took Leo in his mouth, sucking the tip and Leo let out a cry. "Fuck. Fuck. Yeah, that's good."

By the time Nick was bobbing shallowly over him, Leo was flushed and his balls ached. "Hang on, hang on," he pleaded.

Nick froze, lifting off with a soft, wet pop. "Everything okay?"

"Yeah, just need a sec," he said with a breathless laugh. "Or this'll be over before it gets started."

Nick sat back and Leo wiggled out of his sweater, tossing it on the nearby couch. "I'm a little hot." The fire was roaring now, the room warm and cozy.

Nick dragged a hand down his chest, gaze appreciative. "More than a little."

Leo grinned, charmed by the cheesy joke and the look in Nick's eyes. "Hey, lose your shirt and come here, mister," he said huskily. "I want to touch you too."

Nick stripped the rest of his clothes off and settled on the nest of cushions beside Leo. "Did I do okay?" he asked, searching Leo's face.

"Yeah." Leo smiled. "You were amazing. I was getting *too* close, actually."

"Good." Nick rubbed his thumb across Leo's hip. "Tell me what else you want."

"Um," Leo said, because this could be an awkward conversation. "I want you to fuck me but I am also very full of dinner so … not *that* right now."

Understanding lit Nick's eyes. "Sure. What would feel good?"

"It was hot getting off on you the other day," Leo admitted. "But I'd like it even more if we got off together."

"Show me?" Nick asked.

Leo bent his head, kissing Nick's collarbone. "Lube?"

"Oh, one sec." Nick flipped over, rummaging through the drawer in the coffee table. "Here."

"Is this your usual stash or did you prepare for this?" Leo teased.

"I prepared." Nick looked bashful. "Didn't want to ruin the mood by having to run upstairs bare-assed to grab it if you were up for fooling around by the fire."

God, could he get any more amazing? Leo let out a happy sigh and took the bottle from him. He slicked his hand and scooted closer.

Nick was getting hard too and Leo took them both in his hand, slicking their cocks.

Nick groaned. "Fuck, Leo …"

"Yeah, you like that?" Leo asked, rocking into his fist.

"Fuck. It's *amazing*."

It took a few moments for them to find their rhythm but when they did, Leo's head swam. "Ooh fuck that's good."

"I know." Nick pulled him closer, putting an arm around Leo's waist.

Leo wrapped his leg around Nick's hip, bending it at the knee, as they rocked their hips together.

Panting against each other's mouths, Leo murmured. "You can play with my ass if you want. Just the outside and stuff."

"Yeah, yeah I want," Nick said fervently. "Anything to make you feel good."

Leo smiled, groaning a moment later when Nick brushed slippery fingers between his cheeks. "Fuck yeah that's perfect. Don't stop!"

He stroked their cocks and Nick teased at his entrance. Leo let out a moan when his knuckles brushed Leo's balls.

"Yeah, that's good too," he encouraged and Nick cupped them, his palm slick.

Leo tensed when Nick rolled them in his hand.

"You like that or no?" Nick asked, stilling.

"I *like*," Leo assured him and Nick's eyes lit up and he did it again.

There was something powerfully intense having sex this way, looking deeply into Nick's eyes.

The gentle roll and tug of Nick's hand made Leo's skin heat and he bucked into his fist, dragging his thumb across the head of Nick's cock.

Nick made a desperate noise and then they were pressing together harder, fucking into Leo's fist, pillows shifting under them. It was clumsy and a lot slippery and they both laughed when Leo lost his grip. But it didn't matter. It didn't matter when Nick looked all flushed and happy and full of need.

It was him and Nick and they were together and Nick wanted a future with him and … Leo came with a desperate, strangled shout, pressing his face to Nick's throat as he came in his hand, wet heat coating his fingers and both their stomachs.

Nick pressed the side of his knuckles against Leo's taint and he let out a strangled gasp, the orgasm going on and on until Leo was shaking and had to push Nick's hand away before it became too much.

Leo had the wherewithal to let go of his own cock and focus on Nick's, his grip snug, sliding his thumb over the opening on the head until Nick let out a strangled noise, body bowing as he came, panting against Leo's shoulder.

He gripped Leo's ass, fingers sliding across his skin, breath warm against Leo's collarbone. "Leo," he murmured and it sent a rush of warmth through Leo's body.

After, when Leo was so wrung out his bones had melted into a puddle of bliss, he rubbed his nose against Nick's. "Thank you," he whispered.

"For what?" Nick drew a hand up Leo's back but it was tacky with drying lube and they smiled at each other in amusement.

"For … *everything*," Leo said quietly. "For being my perfect match."

Smiling, Nick pressed a kiss to his cheek. "Thanks for moving to town and building my website."

"I *knew* I was going to find love here," Leo said happily, smiling up at the ceiling, his future playing out in a dazzling array of happy possibilities before his eyes.

CHAPTER EIGHTEEN

When Nick finally had feeling in his legs again, he rolled onto his back with a groan. They'd made an unholy mess. There was lube and cum everywhere, coating their bodies and the pillows and the pieces of clothing they'd use to mop up.

"I think next time we should use a bed," he admitted, glancing over at Leo.

He giggled, sitting up. His hair was a mess and he had a fading crease on his cheek from the pillow. He looked so amazing Nick's chest ached.

"I love you," he whispered thickly, his eyes suddenly, unexpectedly wet.

Leo blinked and threw himself forward, landing against Nick's chest so hard it knocked a surprised gasp from him.

"I love you too," Leo whispered against Nick's throat.

Nick hugged him tightly, trembling, overwhelmed by the emotion sweeping over him.

"Hey," Leo shifted to look him in the eye. "Are these good tears?"

Nick nodded, wiping them away with the back of his hand. "When I lost Nicole," he rasped. "I thought it was the end. I thought … I thought I'd found my happily ever after and I'd have to be okay with never finding it again. I thought I'd grow old alone."

Sadness flickered over Leo's face so Nick reached out and took his hand. "But I was wrong. I was so wrong and I'm so glad of it. Because now there's *you*, and Leo …" He shook his head, letting out a breathless little laugh. "You have no idea how happy you make me. How *alive* I feel again."

"Oh, Nick …" Leo whispered.

For a few moments, they stared into each other's eyes. Leo shivered.

"Shit," Nick said, realizing the fire had burned down to ashes and the room was growing cold. He snagged a throw blanket from the couch and wrapped it around Leo's shoulders. "Go upstairs and shower. I'll throw some stuff in the wash and be up shortly."

"You sure?" Leo hesitated. "I could help."

"I'm sure," Nick said firmly. "It won't take me long. Take a nice hot shower and get ready for bed. Help yourself to anything you need."

"Thanks." Leo kissed his cheek, then stood, the throw wrapped around his shoulders like a cape. It fluttered behind him as he opened the French doors, shooting a small smile at Nick before he disappeared.

For a moment, Nick sat there, soaking in the moment, more content than he had been in years.

He was getting cold too and stood, slipping on a pair of boxer briefs. It didn't take long to poke at the ashes, spreading the embers to cool, then close the glass doors on the fireplace. He stripped the covers off the dirty pillows and gathered their remaining clothes into a ball to carry downstairs.

He started a load of laundry, pausing when he caught a glimpse of the desk he'd bought for Leo's Christmas gift through the door to his workshop. He'd almost ruined the surprise yesterday when he was giving Leo a tour of the place but he'd remembered just in time.

So far, he'd gotten the hardware and thick varnish off the desk, then repaired the feet. He still had to do a thorough sanding and fresh polyurethane finish, plus new hardware.

With a week to go before Christmas, he'd have to hurry, but he wanted to see the look on Leo's face when he saw the restored desk.

But Nick was freezing now—standing nearly naked and barefoot in an unfinished basement in the middle of December—so he jogged up the stairs.

Nick hummed to himself as he fed Jelly her nighttime meal, listening to her happy chirrups, and eagerly anticipating the hot shower in his future. If he was lucky, Leo would still be in it.

He quickly tidied the kitchen, then set the dishwasher to run.

When Nick was finished with his nightly chores, he walked up to the second floor.

He froze in the doorway, looking at Leo, lying in bed with his nose buried in a paperback book, Jelly curled up beside him. He petted her absently, pausing only to flick to the next page in his story before settling a hand on her again.

Like something he'd seen a thousand times before.

Leo looked nothing like Nicole really. And yes, they both liked books and cats and those were surface similarities but there was so much more to it. Something *special* about both of them. Something vibrant and loving and kind.

Leo wasn't a replacement for the love Nick had lost but the dawning of a new, hopeful future. Someone who'd shaken him up and reminded him the world was a beautiful place and there were wonderful people in it. Someone who'd reminded him love was infinite, as long as he was open to it.

"Oh," he whispered, overwhelmed.

Leo glanced up, beaming. "Hi!"

"Hi," Nick said, leaning against the doorframe and taking in the cozy sight, breathless with the feelings coursing through him.

"Just hanging out in the doorway, huh?" Leo asked, clearly amused.

"For a minute, yeah." He wanted to soak this in so he'd never forget the moment. Hopefully it would become ordinary in time. In a year or two, when every night was like this, he didn't want to lose the wonder he felt.

The miraculous joy of a life with someone he loved.

In the morning, Leo awoke with Jelly on one side but an empty bed on the other. He frowned.

He'd slept sandwiched between them, cozy and warm in Nick's arms, but the sheets were cool beside him and Nick was nowhere in sight. Nick had promised to play hooky from matchmaking work today, even though it was a Wednesday.

So where had he gone?

With a shrug, Leo decided he was probably downstairs in his office or something and got out of bed. Maybe he'd decided to do some work while he waited for Leo to wake up.

Leo used the bathroom, then found a pile of clothes on the dresser with a note saying, *Borrow me.* Plus a heart with Nick's name.

"Aww," Leo said, happily putting on Nick's underwear, pajama pants, cozy tee, sweater, and socks. Jelly gave him a disgruntled look when he shooed her off the bed and made it.

Leo bounced down the steps, excited to start his day with Nick. But, to his surprise, Nick was nowhere to be found. Leo called out his name but there was no answer.

The living room was neat and tidy—all of the pillows with their freshly washed covers back in place—but empty. He couldn't find Nick in the kitchen or home gym.

"Where did you go?" Leo muttered under his breath as he stuck his head in Nick's office. Maybe he'd gone to pick up breakfast? That seemed like a Nick thing to do. But it was strange he hadn't left a note.

Leo turned, freezing at the sight of the photo on Nick's desk. It was of him. He glanced around, wondering where the photo of Nick and Nicole's wedding had gone and he found it on a shelf with her books. He smiled, liking that Nick hadn't hidden it away. It was a part of Nick's life. His history. Leo didn't want to erase Nicole from Nick's life at all.

"I've got this from here," he promised the woman in the photo quietly. "I'll take good care of him."

He walked to the desk and picked up the photo there, studying it. It wasn't from the shoot they'd done for his matchmaking profile. He frowned, wondering when Nick had taken it. In the photo, Leo was dressed warmly and it had been taken at night. There were colorful lights on his face and …

"Ohh," Leo said softly, putting the pieces together. It had been taken at the tree lighting, when Nick had barely known him. He'd taken the most beautiful photograph of Leo he'd ever seen of himself.

Leo's throat went thick. "You romantic," he whispered.

Jelly yowled, winding around his ankles and Leo laughed softly, setting down the frame. "You aren't supposed to be in here," he reminded her, lifting her and cuddling her against his chest. "Let's go find your guy. *Our* guy, I guess."

He smiled goofily to himself as he closed the office door behind him. He made a lap of the house but Nick was nowhere to be found. There had been a sprinkling of snow overnight and there were no telltale tire tracks or footprints in the driveway so clearly he hadn't left.

"Where *are* you?" he muttered. He wasn't worried Nick had freaked out and bailed. Leo knew he was in this for the long haul. Besides, it was his fucking house.

"The basement, maybe?" he asked Jelly, who he was still carrying around.

She butted her head against his chin in answer, so he kissed the top of her head and tried the door.

"Nick?" he called out.

"Leo? Don't come down here!"

Nick sounded panicked and Leo frowned, confused as Nick appeared at the bottom of the stairs, dusting his clothing off.

"Okay?" Leo said with a small laugh.

Nick jogged up the stairs. "Seriously. Please don't go down there."

"Well, *that's* ominous sounding," Leo teased.

"No. No. It's not ominous. There's just something I don't want you to see."

"Umm, should I be worried? Are you a serial killer or something?"

Nick chuckled. "Uhh, no. I promise I do not have any bodies hidden anywhere. I have a surprise for you and it's down there and I don't want you to see it until Christmas."

"*Oh.*" Leo laughed softly. "Well, that's acceptable." He kissed Nick's cheek. "I like surprises."

"Good." He petted Jelly. "Now, how about we get you fed?"

"Me or Jelly?" Leo asked, stepping back so Nick could shut the basement door.

"Both of you. I was thinking we'd make breakfast, then have a lazy day together. Maybe build another fire, watch a movie …"

"I love that idea!" Leo said happily. "I wanna watch the one that was filmed here last year."

"*Merry Litmas*?" Nick asked, walking toward the kitchen.

"Yeah! That one." Leo followed, trying not to ogle Nick's ass in pajama pants. "Have you seen it?"

"I have but I don't mind rewatching. It's cheesy but good."

"I like cheese," Leo said.

Nick laughed, pouring food into Jelly's bowl. "I know you do."

Jelly launched herself out of Leo's arms and began gobbling her food.

"Well, now that she's fed," Nick said. "How about breakfast for us?"

"Sold."

Leo helped, so it wasn't long before they sat down to fluffy, cheesy scrambled eggs, toast, and bacon.

After, they turned on the Christmas tree lights, snuggled up in front of a roaring fire, and queued up "*Merry Litmas*" on the TV.

They'd barely made it ten minutes into the movie when Nick's phone rang. "Shit," he muttered, glancing at the screen. "I need to get this."

"Want me to pause?" Leo asked, reaching for the remote.

"Nah. Keep going."

He disappeared out the French doors and Leo frowned, then looked at Jelly who had curled up in his lap.

"He is mysterious sometimes, isn't he?" he asked and the cat cracked one eye open, then closed it again.

"Ford? Are you okay?" Nick frowned, worried that his brother-in-law had called him out of nowhere.

"Yeah, I …" Ford cleared his throat. "Sorry for calling out of the blue. I had a question."

"Okay."

"It's about your matchmaking service."

"Oh, did you want to sign up? I've got a new website for it. I'd love to help match you with someone."

"No, I … I was just wondering about one of your clients."

"Well, that's confidential."

"It's just that Mason is a … friend of mine. I want to make sure this date he's going on is safe."

Nick frowned, puzzled. "I vet all my clients, and they always meet at a public place. Mason will be fine. He's a sweetheart, and he totally deserves love. Honestly, I think the date I've got lined up is going to find him adorable."

"You've got a date for him? Who?"

"I can't tell you that," Nick said gently.

"Then tell me when and where, at least. So I can go … keep an eye on them and make sure Mason is okay."

Nick's frown deepened. "Sorry, can't do that either."

"Then what good are you?" Ford snapped.

"Wow," Nick said quietly, rubbing at his chest. That hurt.

"Sorry, I didn't mean that." Ford's tone turned remorseful.

"Maybe you did. This is the first time you've wanted to talk to me in a long time," Nick pointed out.

"Yeah, I know. Shit. I just … Seeing you just makes me think of Nicole and how she's not beside you. It's hard."

"I know," he said softly. "It hasn't been easy for me either."

"Yeah. I've been a miserable bastard to everyone for too long. I'm starting to see that."

"Charlie has been good for you," Nick said, because that had been very clear when he saw them at the bookstore.

"Yeah, she has."

"And Mason?" Nick suggested. "Has he been good for you too?"

Because it was starting to feel like Ford's worry about who Mason was dating was more than concern about a friend.

There was silence for a moment. "I think so. Maybe. I don't know. I'm kind of confused."

Nick chuckled. "I kind of thought you might be. You seemed like maybe you were a little upset he was going on a date?"

"Uh, well … I shouldn't be."

"Why not?"

"I mean, I'm— You know I'm straight, Nick. I was married to LuAnne."

"And I was married to your sister, but you've always known I was bi. You *can* be attracted to men and women. I'm living proof."

Ford snorted. "Yeah, I've heard the rumors about you and that new guy. The whole town has been talking about how you're moving on."

Nick winced at the hint of bitterness in Ford's voice. Was *that* what this was really about? He took a moment, trying to figure out how to word what he wanted to say. "I'll always love Nicole. You know that, right?"

"Yeah."

"And I think she'd want me to move on. She'd want you to be happy too, and if Mason makes you happy …"

"I kind of screwed up," Ford said. "I don't know if he'd want to date me now."

"Well, I don't normally do this, but … If you want to know how he feels about you, I think I can help. Here's what you'd need to do …"

Leo *did* pause the movie when Nick returned a short while later, because he looked … odd.

"Hey, what is it?" Leo asked, concerned.

Nick sat beside him, falling heavily onto the couch. "Uhh, that was Ford Donnely calling."

"Your former brother-in-law?"

"Yeah. That's the one. He, uh, he said he'd heard we were dating."

"Oh no." Leo reached out to touch Nick's arm. "Was he upset? I can imagine it would be hard to see you moving forward with your life."

"Well, that's what I expected at first," Nick said.

Leo squeezed his arm, listening intently as Nick described the conversation.

"*Interesting*," Leo said when he got to the part about Ford's feelings for Mason.

Nick shot him a faint grin, nodding. "I guess he's had an *awakening* recently. There's a guy he has feelings for. He was worked up about the idea of me setting up this guy on a date with someone else. I suggested that if he was so worried, maybe he should go out with him himself."

"Aww, *cute*," Leo said. "And he seems open to it?"

"Yes, I think so," Nick said slowly. "He's figuring things out but it sounds like it."

"Well, good for him. I'm glad he reached out to you."

"Yeah, I was surprised. It's been so long and it was awkward when we ran into each other at the bookstore. Honestly, I didn't think he wanted anything to do with me."

"But it seemed like a positive conversation today?"

"Yeah. Yeah, it really was. I don't think it magically *fixed* everything but it's a step in the right direction. Like maybe we could repair our relationship."

"That's important to you, isn't it?"

"Yeah, it is," Nick said roughly. "He was like a brother to me. Even if we can't get back to that point, I'd love it if we could be friends."

Leo threaded their fingers together. "Well, I hope it works out."

"Thanks." Nick let out a sigh, placing his phone on the coffee table, then settling close to Leo. "Shall we get back to our movie now? I can rewind."

"Yeah, sounds good."

A few moments later, Leo rested his head on Nick's shoulder and let himself get swept away in the holiday romance playing out on screen.

He'd already found his happily ever after. But there could never be too much love this time of year.

CHAPTER NINETEEN

Nick paced anxiously as he waited for Leo's parents to arrive on Christmas Day.

Anneliese and Randal Fenner were staying at Gingerbread Cottage—the quaint little bed and breakfast on St. Nick Avenue. They'd arrived on the twenty-third and Leo had spent the day with them, showing them around town and taking them to shops and events.

Leo had come with Nick to his family's Christmas Eve celebration yesterday at Nick's parents' house. They'd had an enjoyable afternoon and evening, eating dinner, opening gifts, and drinking eggnog and eating cookies by the fireplace. His parents, along with Heather and Edie and their kids, had quickly been smitten with Leo—because how could anyone *not* be?—and they'd all agreed Leo was perfect for him.

But today Nick would meet Leo's family and damn was he nervous.

"Hey." Leo wrapped his arms around Nick's waist. "Why are you freaking out?"

Apparently, he wasn't hiding his anxiety well.

"What if they don't like me?"

Leo chuckled, pressing a kiss to the back of his neck. "Why on earth wouldn't they?"

"I'm an old, widowed guy?"

Leo snorted. "You're *thirty-eight*. You're hardly an octogenarian. And it's not your fault you're widowed."

"I know, but …"

"Hey," Leo said, coaxing Nick to turn. "You're a great guy and you make me happy. They'll see that immediately."

"You think so?" he said, suddenly doubtful.

"Even if you weren't amazing, my parents know I had a guy *scam me out of money*. And that I had a date with a dude who took me out for the first time to *Hooters*. The bar is really fucking low, Nick."

"Hooters?" Nick asked, blinking.

"Yeah, Hooters. I mean, the wings are decent but women in skimpy clothing is kinda lost on me, you know? And the guy knew I wasn't bi."

Nick grimaced. "Yikes."

"Yeah, you really don't have any reason to worry."

"But I walked out on you—"

Leo shrugged. "When I talked to them about you recently, I explained your history. They understand why you got spooked about falling in love for the first time since you lost your wife."

Nick opened his mouth to reply, when there was a knock on the door.

"Stop worrying," Leo said firmly. He pressed a quick, hard kiss to Nick's mouth, then pulled back, striding over to open the front door.

Nick pasted a smile on his face and prepared himself to face an interrogation from Leo's parents. But the moment they stepped into the house, exclaiming over the original details of the house and greeting him warmly, he realized he'd been an idiot.

These were the people who had raised Leo. They were bubbly, friendly, kind Midwesterners, determined to see the best in people.

Anneliese was short, round and blonde, with curly hair and a bright smile.

"You must be Nick!" She squeezed him in a tight hug. "Thank you so much for inviting us over. Your home is lovely!"

"Oh," he said, feeling dazed. "Thank you. I am glad you could come."

Randal, who had Leo's sandy brown hair and wiry build, chuckled. "It's not often we can get away from the farm but after Leo moved here, we couldn't resist the opportunity to take a vacation."

"Glad you did," Nick said, holding out a hand. "It's great to meet you."

Randal shook, pulling him into a big, back-slapping hug too. "It's already been worth the drive," he said beaming.

"Next year I hope you'll both come to Wisconsin," Annelise said. "So we can all be together. Adam and Jason send their love by the way, Leo. Your brothers are so mad they don't get to meet your boyfriend."

Leo smiled. "We can do a video chat later and introduce Nick to them."

"Please come in," Nick coaxed, the tension in his shoulders loosening at the friendly onslaught of conversation.

"Yeah, we want to give you a tour!" Leo said. "Take your boots and coat off."

"Wait." Randal held up a hand. "We've gotta get some presents out of the truck first."

After the Fenners hauled in gifts, they stripped off their outerwear, revealing jeans and festive Christmas sweaters.

Nick hung their coats on the pegs by the door and a lump rose in his throat at the sight of the jumble of colorful jackets. For so long, it had just been him. He'd sorely missed the signs of life in this house. When he'd had a partner to share the holidays with an extended family around.

Leo excitedly chattered to his parents, showing off Nick's house, and he thought it wouldn't be too long before he asked Leo to move in with him. If Leo needed more time, that was okay. Nick would give him whatever he needed.

But life was short and Nick had every intention of filling his with as much joy as possible. And Leo Fenner was his joy.

"See, I *knew* you were worrying for no good reason," Leo whispered, hooking his arm in Nick's bent elbow as they directed Leo's parents toward Nick's home office. "They love you."

Nick smiled. "It's been like twenty minutes. I think it's a little too soon for them to love me."

"It didn't take me long to fall for you," Leo said cheerfully. "I was already smitten by the time I left our first meeting."

Nick gave him a thoughtful look. "I think I was heading that direction too, even if I didn't want to admit it."

"So how is your matchmaking business going?" Anneliese asked as Nick pushed open the door to his office.

"Pretty well," Nick said. "Though I did have one spectacular failure."

"I'm not a failure," Leo protested, pouting.

Laughing, Nick pulled him close. "No! Not *you*. I meant Jett." Nick glanced at Leo's parents. "One of my clients started dating a mutual friend of ours."

"I helped get them together," Leo said smugly. "Apparently Nick's not the *only* matchmaker around here."

Randal grimaced. "I think two jobs might be enough, son. You don't need a third."

Leo chuckled. "Coming from the guy who's a farmer and on the school board and town council …" He shot his dad a pointed look.

He grinned, shrugging.

"Speaking of the matchmaking, how many dates did it take

for you to find love, Leo?" Anneliese asked. "I've always found the process fascinating."

"Ten," Nick replied, just as Leo said, "Twelve."

"It was ten," Nick protested.

"No, *twelve*. I had five dates with other dudes and I called you after all of them, and seven were with you."

Nick frowned, ticking them off on his fingers. "The reindeer meet and greet and sleigh ride, the wine tasting we went to, the boat ride to the falls, the antique shopping and hockey date, then the romantic dinner and movie by the fire. That's five."

"You forgot the photoshoot plus lunch at Frosty's and the time I got ghosted by the guy with the shellfish allergy and we watched the parade together," Leo countered, holding up two fingers.

"Those weren't dates!" Nick protested.

"Weren't they though?" Leo asked, giggling. "Even if we—and by we, I mostly mean you—didn't admit it at the time, they were totally dates."

Nick gave him a rueful smile. "You're right."

"Twelve dates," Annelise said, nodding. "That sounds like the perfect amount!"

"Oh, that reminds me, Leo. I got a text from Ford saying he and Mason are together." Nick glanced at Leo's parents again. "My former brother-in-law just started seeing someone recently."

"Aww. Well that's lovely."

"It really is." Nick beamed. "We—we had a rough patch after Nicole died but it feels really good that we're working on our relationship again."

"Oh that's wonderful." Annelise said. "Family dynamics can be so tricky sometimes but I think it's always good if you can mend fences whenever you're able."

She sobered. "By the way, I was very sorry to hear about your wife."

"Thank you," Nick said gravely. "It was difficult. But I am glad it didn't keep me from falling in love again."

Anneliese reached out and touched his arm. "We are too. Leo can't stop talking about you. I haven't seen him this happy in years."

"I'm right here, Mom," Leo said, feeling exasperated, but mostly glad that his parents could see how good Nick was for him. Not that he'd ever doubted it but … it was still nice.

She grinned. "I know you are."

"I like your desk," Randal said. "Did that come with the house, Nick?"

He brightened, telling them about Merry Memories and the trip he and Leo had taken recently.

"Ugh, I should have bought that desk we looked at," Leo said with a regretful sigh. "Maybe I'll go back and get it next week. Hopefully it's still there."

Nick shot him an odd look but before Leo could ask what that was about, Anneliese gasped, picking up the photo of Leo on Nick's desk.

"Oh! Did you take this?" She looked at Nick.

He nodded. “Yes. I’m an amateur photographer and I took it at the tree lighting shortly after Leo moved to town.”

“It’s *beautiful.* Could we get a copy to put on our mantle?”

“Of course. I can send you an email with a bunch of photos I took of him for his matchmaking profile as well.”

“Yeah, it’s not like I’m going to need that anymore.” Leo kissed Nick’s cheek.

Nick smiled. “Well, what do you say we all go relax by the fire?”

As they left Nick’s office, Leo snagged Jelly, who had snuck in when no one was looking.

Anneliese and Randal exclaimed over how cute she was and Nick told the story about how she got her name. Leo smiled as he followed them down the hall.

“Make yourselves comfortable,” Nick told Leo’s parents as he ushered them into the living room. “I’ll get the fire going.”

“And I’ll grab the hot cocoa and treats!” Leo said, setting Jelly on the couch beside his mom, who reached out to pet her.

“Thanks.” Nick shot him a smile.

This morning, they’d made up a big batch of cocoa in a slow cooker and had cookies and pastries from Ginger’s Breads, so it didn’t take Leo long to assemble a tray. But to his surprise, when he carried it into the living room, his dad and Nick were nowhere to be found.

“Where’d they go?” he asked, mystified.

“To get something from the basement,” his mom said, standing to help him set the tray on the coffee table.

"Ahh. I think that's my gift," Leo admitted. "Nick told me I wasn't allowed down there. For a minute I wondered if he was a serial killer."

She laughed. "Well, let's hope not! For what it's worth, he seems like a very nice man to me."

"You don't mind the age difference?" Leo asked quietly. He wasn't worried, but Nick had been and he wanted to be sure.

Anneliese shook her head. "No. It's clear he adores you. I'd feel different if you were seventeen but you're a grown man."

Leo made a face. "If I'd been seventeen it would be sketchy as hell."

"Exactly. You've always had a good head on your shoulders though. You've made some very grown-up, smart decisions in the past few years and your father and I are very proud of you."

"Aww, thanks," Leo said, smiling as he took a seat beside his mom. "That means a lot to me."

"Close your eyes, Leo!" Nick called out from the hall.

"What?"

His mom clapped her hand over his eyes. "They're closed!" she replied.

Leo sputtered but he didn't push her hand away. He'd meant it when he told Nick he liked surprises.

Someone grunted, then there was a muffled oath before Nick said, "Open them, Leo!"

His mom lifted her hand away and he blinked to see a gleaming wooden desk standing a few feet away, sporting a big red bow. He studied it for a moment before his jaw dropped. "Is that … is that the one from Merry Memories?"

Nick beamed. "It is."

"Holy shit! It's gorgeous." Leo stepped around the coffee table to inspect the desk. "You did a ton of work on this."

"I did." Nick chuckled. "Honestly, I wasn't sure if I'd get it done in time but I put the final coat of polyurethane finish on the other day while you were out with your parents, then added the hardware this morning."

"It's *stunning*," Leo whispered, brushing his fingertips across the satiny surface. "Wow. I love it."

He turned and threw his arms around Nick, kissing him hard. He tensed for a second before he wrapped Leo up tightly in a hug and kissed him back.

"I'm glad," Nick said, smiling when he pulled away.

"Thank you. This was so sweet of you. How did you even get it home? And down to the basement for that matter!"

"Liam," Nick said.

Leo looked blank. "Liam?"

"Liam Barlowe. He owns Merry Memories."

"Oh!" Leo chuckled. "He wasn't very friendly, was he?"

"Oh, that's just Liam," Nick said with a shrug. "We went to school together and he's always been a loner. He took over the shop after his grandparents died a few years ago. I think he preferred when he only had to run their online shop. He's not a people-person. Nice guy though. I was prepared to lug the desk down the stairs to the basement but he offered to help."

"Aww, well that was sweet. And if I haven't said it yet, thank you for the desk. I love it," Leo said earnestly.

"Good. That makes me happy." Nick squeezed his hips.

"*You* make me happy," Leo countered.

"That goes both ways."

"They're so sweet together," Anneliese whispered. "Look at them, Randal. It reminds me of us when we were young."

Leo jerked in surprise because he'd kinda forgotten his parents were there. He pulled away, his cheeks warming.

"If you need help getting the desk up to Leo's apartment, let me know," Randal said, clearing his throat.

Leo bit his lip, glancing over at Nick. "I thought maybe it could stay here."

"Yeah?"

"I mean, I'm not inviting myself to move in," he said, laughing awkwardly.

Nick smiled. "You *could*. Whenever you're ready."

"Well, let's give it a few months," Leo said, because he didn't have any doubts about Nick or being with him, but it was good to figure out each other's bad habits and stuff before they started living together. "But I could use the desk here until we make it official?"

"Yeah. Yeah, sounds good to me," Nick said softly, his voice rough. He brushed his lips across Leo's temple.

Leo leaned into him and let out a contented sigh, soaking in the moment.

"Well, I don't think it's a *desk* but I saw a package labeled with my name earlier and I'd like to open it," Randal said, rubbing his hands together.

"Randy!" Anneliese thwacked his side. "Give the boys a moment."

Leo chuckled. "No, we don't want to let our cocoa get cold. Let's open some Christmas gifts!"

After, as Leo watched his mother clear away the tray and his father help Nick gather up discarded wrapping paper and tissue, dragging a ribbon away from Jelly who kept batting at it, Leo let out a contented sigh.

The desk was an amazing gift, but *this* was the Christmas present he treasured most.

EPILOGUE

"Where are you going?" Nick rasped as Leo tiptoed around his side of bed later that week.

"Sorry," Leo whispered. "Didn't mean to wake you."

"It's okay." Nick wrapped an arm around his waist and pulled him close, tumbling him onto the bed. "But I had plans for you."

Leo shot him a curious look. "What *kind* of plans?"

"Touching every inch of you." Nick grinned. "Kissing you everywhere. Sliding inside of you until you cry out my name. Those kind of plans."

"Oh. *Those* kind, huh?" Leo blinked.

"If you want."

"Hell yeah I do." Leo threw back the sheets and stretched out next to Nick.

Nick laughed, loving that Leo was so enthusiastic about nearly everything he suggested, in or out of bed.

"Stay here," Nick said. "I've gotta brush my teeth."

When he returned, feeling all minty fresh, Leo was stretched out on the bed naked, with two fingers in his ass. Nick fumbled the hand towel he'd been carrying.

"What happened to taking my time?" Nick teased, leaning against the bathroom doorframe. He'd planned something a lot slower and more thorough, but he wasn't exactly mad about the sight in front of him.

"I got impatient," Leo said with a grin.

"I was gone for three minutes!"

"I know. Way too long." Leo stared through his lashes, pressing deeper, his mouth dropping open with a gasp.

Nick pushed off the doorframe and stalked over to the bed. "Well, at least let me *help*."

"Okay." Leo gasped. "If you insist."

Nick settled on the bed behind him, running his hands up and down Leo's flanks for a moment, savoring the feel of his soft skin and the taut muscles below. He pressed a kiss to Leo's shoulder, then reached for the lube.

Leo slid his fingers free and Nick replaced them with his own. In minutes, Leo was writhing against him, head bowed, panting and pushing back on Nick's fingers.

With every day that passed, Nick learned more about what Leo loved. How to drive him crazy. He twisted his fingers, brushing his other hand against Leo's balls.

Leo buried his face against the pillows, gasping out a muffled, "Nick!"

"Yeah? Do you need something?"

"You," Leo begged, turning his head. "C'mon."

"I could drag this out," Nick teased, though from the feel of his own cock, he'd give in quickly.

Leo pouted. "You're so mean!"

"Am I? I thought I was a nice guy."

"Not at the moment."

Laughing and dizzyingly in love with Leo, Nick slid his fingers free, wiped them on the towel, then rolled on a condom.

"I'll be nice."

Leo groaned low and long when Nick pushed inside him. And although he might not have had time to touch and kiss him before, he did so as he moved slowly inside Leo, tasting his skin, touching every inch of him like he'd promised.

And when Leo came, crying out his name, Nick wrapped him in his arms and held him close. "I love you," he whispered thickly. "I love you."

Because he could never say that too often. Life was short and love should be treasured.

"Welcome!" Nick said a few hours later. "C'mon in!"

Joel and Hayden stepped inside and Hayden immediately started laughing. "Uhh, Leo, you might want to fix your hair and Nick, you might want to fix your zipper there."

"Shit!" Nick fumbled for it, his face warming. They'd started making out on the couch and lost track of time. "Sorry. We uh, got distracted waiting for people to arrive."

Joel grinned and clapped Nick on the shoulder. "Happens to the best of us."

Before Nick could say anything else, he spotted some more familiar faces coming up the walk. "Uncle Nick!" his nephew Sammi called out, waving. "Hi!"

"Hi!" Nick crouched down and held out his arms. "I've missed you."

Sammi giggled but wrapped his arms around Nick's neck. "You saw me on Christmas Eve!"

"Too long!" Nick kissed his cheek.

Mimi launched herself at him too and Nick hugged her, wrapping both kids up in his arms. His sister-in-law, Edie, smiled as she kicked off her shoes, talking about something with Leo.

But he tensed a few moments later when Ford Donnely and Mason West came up the sidewalk with Ford's stepdaughter, Charlie, walking between them, holding both of their hands.

Nick had been surprised but pleased when Ford had agreed to come to the snowman building and board games get-together he and Leo had organized after the Fenners headed back to Wisconsin.

Ford seemed stiff when he greeted Nick and his smile looked slightly forced as he shook Leo's hand. Charlie hung back too, looking unsure, but it wasn't long before Mimi and Sammi befriended her and Heather and Edie drew Ford and Mason into conversation.

Everyone trooped out into the backyard to play in the freshly fallen snow and at one point, Nick stood beside Ford, unsure of what to say.

"Uh, how'd you and Leo meet?" Ford asked.

"Well …" Nick said. "He built my website and I was supposed to match him with someone but … I accidentally fell in love with him myself."

Ford chuckled, his gaze drifting to Mason. "That happens."

"I'm really glad you came today," Nick admitted.

"I am too. And I'm sorry I—I'm sorry I got so distant after Nicole's death. I just didn't know how to be around you without hurting for her …"

"I am sorry too." Nick's throat went thick, remembering the days after her death. "I loved your sister so much."

"You did. I know that." Ford said roughly. "I should have tried harder. We could have supported each other more. I'm sorry, man."

"I appreciate the apology. I know there's a lot more I could have done too."

Ford nodded. "You seem happy now."

Nick smiled at Leo, who was being pelted with snowballs fired by all three kids. "I am."

They fell silent for a few moments, watching the mayhem.

"Nicole would be glad you have him," Ford said softly. "And glad you're doing the matchmaking. It's a nice tribute to her." He glanced at Mason, who was talking to Joel and Hayden. "My sister would be glad we're both happy now."

Nick smiled. "She would."

He liked to think maybe Nicole had a hand in his and Ford's happiness right now. A little bit of Christmas magic, maybe.

"C'mon, Nick!" Leo called out. "I need help! Don't let them gang up on me this way!"

"Gotta go rescue my boyfriend," he said with a shrug at Ford, who just smiled and nodded.

Nick ran across the yard, laughing, his heart light and free as he tackled Leo into the snow and kissed him.

"Merry Christmas," he said, looking down into Leo's pink-cheeked face.

"Christmas is over," Leo protested.

A snowball landed on Nick's upper arm and he glanced over to see a giggling Charlie duck behind Sammi.

Family. Love. Nick really had it all, didn't he?

"It's always Christmas in Christmas Falls," he told Leo, brushing their lips together. "Especially when I'm with you."

THE END

I hope you enjoyed Nick & Leo's story! I really loved writing it. If you're able, please leave a review. I appreciate it so much.

Haven't read Joel & Hayden's story yet? Find ***Scrooge You!*** here.

Ready for more of Christmas Falls: Season 2? Keep reading to find links to the entire series.

MORE CHRISTMAS FALLS

SEASON 2

Don't miss a single Christmas Falls: Season 2 story! Find them all on Amazon & Kindle Unlimited.

The Snuggle is Real by DJ Jamison
Flake It Til You Make It by Beth Bolden
12 Dates of Christmas by Brigham Vaughn
Here Comes Santa Paws by Lee Blair
Under the Mistle-Foe by Rye Cox
Christmas Beau by Amy Aislin
No Business Like Snow Business by J.A. Rock & Lisa Henry
Frost Impressions by Kelly Fox
Promise Yule Be Mine by Rhys Everly
Mingle All the Way by Hayden Hall

BRIGHAM'S BOOKS

Relationship Goals

You can't fake great hockey—but *love* is a totally different game.

What can you expect from the series?

- great hockey
- fake relationships
- real love (eventually)

The Husband Game: Hockey Captain Wed in Secret Vegas Ceremony – Partner's Identity Remains a Mystery.

The Head Game: Defenseman Rushed to Hospital After In-Game Fall—Mystery Beau Revealed?

The Waiting Game: Fisher Cats' Hale and Brewer Engaged: College Sweethearts or Fake Relationship?

The Home Game: Matty Carlson Playing House with Local Schoolteacher?

The Blame Game: Fiery Rescue: Fisher Cats Player Heating Up the Sheets with Handsome Stranger?

Christmas Falls Shared World

Christmas Falls is a multi-author M/M romance series set in a small town that thrives on enough holiday charm to rival any Hallmark movie.

Find Season One stories from DJ Jamison, Jacki James, Amy Aislin, Beth Bolden, Sammi Cee, Casey Cox, Hayden Hall, Rye Cox, and myself here.

Scrooge You! - Hayden Bradley hates Christmas and everything to do with it …

Find Season Two stories from DJ Jamison, Beth Bolden, Lee Blair, Rye Cox, Amy Aislin, Lisa Henry, J.A. Rock, Kelly Fox, Rhys Everly, Hayden Hall, and myself here.

12 Dates of Christmas - Leo Fenner needs a Christmas miracle.

All books in the shared world can be read as standalones.

Rules of the Game

Join the pro hockey players who fight hard and love hard in the Rules of the Game Universe.

The chronological reading order is *Road Rules, Bending the Rules, Changing the Rules, Unwritten Rules, Rules of Engagement, and Breaking the Rules.*

Also available in audio!

Rules of the Game: Evanston River Otters

Road Rules: Rule #1: Don't fall in love with your best friend.

Bending the Rules: Rule #1: Never give up on love.

Changing the Rules: Rule #1: Don't fall in love with your coach.

Unwritten Rules: Rule #1: Don't fall in love with your family's sworn enemy.

Rules of Engagement: Rule #1: Don't fall in love with your brother's best friend.

Breaking the Rules: Rule #1: Don't fall in love with your agent.

Pendleton Bay Books

Visit the fictional small town of Pendleton Bay on the shores of Lake Michigan. All books set in this universe can be read as standalones but characters from other books/series may appear from time to time.

There are currently two series set within the Pendleton Bay Universe.

Naughty in Pendleton Series

A complete m/m romance series set in the town of Pendleton Bay with characters exploring the kinkier side of romance. BDSM elements will appear in all books.

Date in a Pinch: When chemistry teacher Neil gets an unexpected delivery at the high school where he works, he's mortified when his crush, Alexander, sees the contents. Curious but inexperienced with kink, Neil has no idea how to live out his fantasies until the hot lit teacher offers a helping hand.

***Embracing His Shame*:** Forrest, the town's accountant, may look uptight but he's anything but. When he offers the local mechanic, Jarod, an indecent proposal to fulfill his shameful fantasies, Forrest will have to decide if he's willing to give Jarod a chance to show him that he can have love *and* the kink he longs for.

Made to Order: Donovan, head chef at the Hawk Point Tavern, loves to be in charge in the kitchen *and* in the bedroom. Tyler, a former solider, is pretty sure he's straight and definitely only into kink if he's the one dishing it out. Until he and Donovan start butting heads about who is calling the shots …

Flipping the Switch: When Logan, a silver fox Dom looking for experience on a kinky app, stumbles across Jude, a flirty switch who just so happens to be best friend's son, *and* introduces him to a sweet cinnamon roll of a sub named Tony, they heat between them will sizzle hotter than Jude's kitchen. But they'll have to decide if three is the perfect number.

Preston's Christmas Escape: When Hollywood actor Preston gets caught by the paparazzi in a compromising position, he flees to his home state of Michigan to hide out with his former best friend and ex. Reclusive potter Blake is reluctant to let Preston invade his quiet home in the woods but the heat between them can only be denied for so long … (BDSM)

Poly in Pendleton Series

An m/m/f romance series set in the town of Pendleton Bay.

Three Shots: Reeve, a local musician, and Grant, a computer designer, have fun in bed together but pursuing a relationship never feels quite right until they meet tavern owner Rachael and try to figure out how to be poly in the small town of Pendleton Bay.

Peachtree Books

Visit the real life city of Atlanta, Georgia. There are two series set with the Peachtree Universe.

Both series in this universe can be read as standalones but characters from both series do crossover.

The official reading order across both series is *Off-Balance*, *Love in the Balance*, *Trust the Connection*, and *Full Balance.*

The Peachtree Series

Complete, continuous m/m series featuring an age gap, light kink, and found family. *Also available in Italian.*

Off-Balance: Coworkers Russ & Stephen meet over a spilled cup of coffee and navigate the complexities of a nineteen-year age gap, a big difference in income, and the death of Stephen's estranged father.

Love in the Balance: Their story continues as Russ introduces Stephen to his family, searches for his absent mother, and asks Stephen to marry him.

Full Balance: They navigate new challenges as they take in a teenage foster boy named Austin and decide to make him a permanent part of their family.

Peachtree Place

Standalone m/m book in the same universe as *The Peachtree Series*

Trust the Connection: Evan & Jeremy find a love that will heal both their scars in this slow-burn, age-gap romance about living with a disability, believing in yourself, and building the family you always wanted.

The Midwest Series

Complete opposites attract m/m series featuring four couples. Stories intertwine but can be read as standalones.

Bully & Exit: Drama geek Caleb is sure he'll never forgive Nathan, the hockey player who dumped him in high school, until he learns the real reason why in this slow-burn, second-chance new adult romance. Now available in audio.

Push & Pull: Lowell & Brent have nothing in common when they leave on a summer road trip, but by the end, the makeup-wearing fashionista and the macho hockey player will realize they're perfect for each other in this enemies to lovers, slow-burn story about acceptance. Now available in audio.

Touch & Go: Micah, a closeted pro pitcher, and Justin, a laid-back physical therapist, have nothing in common but when Micah blows out his shoulder, he'll have to choose which he wants more: baseball or love? An enemies to lovers, out for you romance. Now available in audio.

Advance & Retreat: When fate brings Ian and Ricky together, a college swimmer will have to figure out how to reached for the gold without losing the sweet hotel manager who lights up the stage as sizzling drag queen Rosie Riveting.

An age gap sports romance with a gender fluid character. Now available in audio.

The West Hills

Standalone m/m series featuring three different couples

The Ghosts Between Us: Losing his brother in a devastating accident sends Chris spiraling into grief. The last person he expects to find comfort in is his brother's secret boyfriend, Elliot, in this slow burn, hurt/comfort romance.

Tidal Series – Co-authored with K Evan Coles

A complete, continuous m/m duology that takes Riley & Carter from best friends to lovers in this slow-burn romance featuring the sons of two wealthy Manhattan families.

Wake: After a decade and a half of lying to himself and everyone around him, Riley slowly come to terms with his sexuality and his feelings for his best friend, Carter, shattering their friendship.

Calm: Carter reaches his own realization and they slowly build the relationship they've been denying for so long.

Speakeasy Series – Co-authored with K Evan Coles

Complete, standalone m/m series featuring characters from the Tidal universe

With a Twist: After Will learns of his estranged father's cancer diagnosis, he returns home and slowly mends fences with him and falls in love with his father's colleague, David. Enemies to lovers, opposites attract, interracial romance.

Extra Dirty: Wealthy, pansexual businessman Jesse is perfectly happy living his life to the fullest with no strings attached, but when he meets Cam, a music teacher and DJ, he'll find that some strings are worth hanging onto in this age-gap, opposites-attract romance.

Behind the Stick: Speakeasy owner and bartender Kyle has taken a break from dating when he's rescued by Harlem firefighter Luka. Interracial romance and hurt/comfort.

Straight Up: When hot, tattooed biker chef Stuart meets quiet and serious Malcolm, they both have secrets they're hiding. Gray ace, bisexual awakening, lingerie kink.

The Williamsville Inn

Standalone m/m holiday romances in a shared universe with Hank Edwards

Snowstorms and Second Chances: Erik and Seth don't hit it off at first, but when a snowstorm leads to them sharing a room at a hotel, Erik discovers a whole new side of himself and his feelings about the holidays. A forced-proximity, bisexual-awakening romance with a second chance at happiness.

The Cupcake Conundrum: Adrian comes face to face with the biggest mistake of his past, Ajay, a hookup who he ghosted on. He'll have to make amends and win Jay's heart back in this single dad, second-chance interracial romance.

Colors Series

A continuous f/f series featuring a bisexual character and opposites attract trope

A Brighter Palette: When Annie, a struggling American freelance writer, meets Siobhán, a successful Irish painter living in Boston, the heat between them is undeniable, but is it enough to build something that will last?

The Greenest Isle: After Siobhán's father has a heart attack, she and Annie travel to Ireland to care for him. Their relationship is tested as they navigate living in a new place and healing old wounds.

Standalone Books

Baby, It's Cold Inside: Meeting Nate's parents doesn't go at all like Emerson planned. But there might be a Christmas miracle for the two of them before the visit is through in this sweet and funny m/m holiday romance.

Bromantic Getaway: Spencer is sure he's straight. But when an off-hand comment sends him tumbling into the realization he's in love with his best friend Devin, he'll have to turn a romantic vacation meant for his ex into the perfect opportunity to grab the love that's always been right in front of them in this best friends to lovers bi awakening m/m romance.

Cabin Fever: Kevin's best friend's dad is definitely off-limits. But he and Drew are about to spend a week alone in a cabin the week before Christmas. And Kevin's never been any good at resisting temptation. An age gap, best friend's father m/m holiday romance.

Also available in audio and in Italian.

Corked: A sommelier and a wine distributor clash in this enemies to lovers, age-gap m/m romance that takes Sean & Lucas from a restaurant in Chicago to owning a winery in Traverse City.

Inked in Blood: **Co-Authored with K Evan Coles** An unexpected event changes the life and death of a sexy, tattooed vampire named Jeff and Santiago, a tattoo artist with a secret. A paranormal, age-gap m/m romance.

Seeking Warmth: When Benny gets out of juvie, he's lost all hope for a future for him or his sister, but the help of his ex-boyfriend Scott will show him that hope and love still exist in this m/m YA novel about second chances.

The Soldier Next Door: When Travis agrees to keep an eye on the guy next door for a few weeks while his parents are out of town, he never expects to fall in love with a soldier heading off to war. An age-gap m/m novella.

ABOUT THE AUTHOR

Brigham Vaughn is on the adventure of a lifetime as a full-time author. She devours books at an alarming rate and hasn't let her short arms and long torso stop her from doing yoga. She makes a killer key lime pie, hates green peppers, and loves wine tasting tours.

A collector of vintage Nancy Drew books and green glass-ware, she enjoys poking around in antique shops and refinishing thrift store furniture. An avid photographer, she dreams of traveling the world and she can't wait to discover everything else life has to offer her.

Her books range from short stories to novellas to novels. They explore gay, bisexual, lesbian, and polyamorous romance in contemporary settings.

Want to read more of Brigham's work, follow her on social media, or stay up to date on new releases and sales via her newsletter?

Click here or scan the QR Code below to find all of Brigham's links on Linktree.

Made in the USA
Monee, IL
27 November 2024

71414313R00173